MICK BOGERMAN'S
WARNING NOTE TO PARENTS:

Hey parents! It's me, Mick Bogerman. I'm here to tell you this story is rated PG for bloodthirstiness and fighting. Girls beware, this is not a sparkling mermaid tale. The mermaid in this story is mean, she will eat you for lunch, and she is scaly gross. The language is standard twelve-year-old name-calling, like dorkhead, boogerbreath, and slug-pie ugly, although I do make a special effort to stay clear of mom insults and potty jokes. As far as romance, you will find absolutely none in this story, because that would be stupid.

So, if you're looking for a wimpy, child-type book, turn away now. But if your kid is not a wimp, likes a heart-pounding scare and chasing down murderous aquatic monsters, then this, dear parent, is the story for your kid.

ALSO BY
MICK BOGERMAN

Slug Pie Story #1:

How to Navigate Zombie Cave and

Defeat Pirate Pete

Coming Soon

Slug Pie Story #3:

How to Destroy the New Girl's Killer

Robot Army

How to Rid Your Swimming Pool of a Bloodthirsty Mermaid

Slug Pie Story #2

How to Rid Your Swimming Pool of a Bloodthirsty Mermaid

Mick Bogerman

SLUG PIE STORIES, LLC

Slug Pie Stories, LLC
8126 West Evergreen Drive
Frankfort, IL 60423

www.slugpiestories.com

Publisher's Note: This is a work of fiction. Names, characters, places, and incidents are a product of the author's imagination. Locales and public names are sometimes used for atmospheric purposes. Any resemblance to actual people, living or dead, or to businesses, companies, events, institutions, or locales is completely coincidental.

Book design © 2013, BookDesignTemplates.com

Cover design © 2014, Kat Powell

Cover illustration © 2014, Kat Powell

Frankfort / Mick Bogerman – First Edition

ISBN 978-0-9903801-3-9

Printed in the United States of America

For Nic, Irina, and Clarissa

Trade Lawn Mows for Pool Swims

PJ'S AFRAID of the lawnmower.

What a goober, right?

But PJ's crazy fear means I get a safe place to teach my little brother, Finley, how to swim.

Me and Finley had a pretty close call fighting off a bunch of pirate zombies last month. Imagine how embarrassing it would've been if Finley had drowned while we were escaping Zombie Cave. Well I swam, he floated, and we both survived. But I spit-swore I'd step up as his swimming instructor.

Over cherry colas, cheeseburgers, and fries drowning in mayonnaise, I bargain seven mowed lawns for seven swims in PJ's ginormous pool. Me and Finley will go to PJ's place the one day a week his Dad's guaranteed to be out of town on business. We seal the deal with a handshake across a table at Gina's Joint.

"We can't take any chances. You can't let my Dad

see you do the mowing." PJ dabs mayonnaise from the corner of his mouth with a napkin.

"No problem." I can do stealth-mode lawn service.

"You and I"—he gives me a quick scan—"we're about the same size. I'll leave my clothes near the cabana for you. And you'll have to wear long sleeves. Just in case my Dad pops home."

I don't say anything when PJ uses the word "pops." I'll save it for later when me and Finley are alone and I give him the recap. Although I'll never be able to mimic PJ's high-pitched snoot. That comes from years of breeding. Which, obviously, I don't got.

The long sleeves will be tough on a hot day, but my tan skin'll never pass for PJ's powdered-donut complexion. I'll have to suffer through, but it'll be worth it.

"And your mom? What about her?" I wonder if she'll pop by too.

"She's at our place in Barcelona all month with my sister." He sips at his straw, pinky hanging in the air like it's gonna take off and fly away.

"Right." I jam a handful of fries in my mouth and try not to spray him with chewed bits when I talk. It's the least I can do. "I don't get it. How come your dad wants you to mow the lawn? Don't you have people? A team of minions looking after your place?"

PJ twists his napkin into a paper cyclone before he sets it on his plate. "We do. But Dad's told them to save the mowing, and the mower, for me." He shudders when he says the word *mower*. "My dad says mowing lawns is how he spent his summers. Builds character."

All mowing lawns ever built for me is a bucketload of tired and a few extra dollars in my pocket, but I don't interrupt.

PJ switches his voice to a creepy baritone. "'If it's good enough for me, it's good enough for my son. I'll not raise a lazy boy with a silver spoon in his mouth who doesn't appreciate the value of a good day's work. Buck up! A little physical labor in the sunshine won't kill you.'"

"OK, OK," I say in my best soothe-the-situation voice. This kid's got daddy issues. Big time. "I'll take care of the physical labor, and you can enjoy the sunshine." I inspect his pasty-pale skin. "Or whatever you like to do in your free time."

PJ doesn't seem the adventurous sort. He wouldn't have survived a minute in Zombie Cave with me and Finley. He's not the kind of kid I normally hang with. But I don't need a new friend. I need a kid with a pool who needs his lawn mowed.

"I have Sea-Monkeys." PJ straightens against the red vinyl booth and flashes a grin.

I've got no clue, but I play along. Try to be nice. "Like Space Monkeys? Fun game. Wii or Xbox?"

"No, no. The real thing. They live in a Sea-Monkey habitat. I'll show you when you and your brother come by tomorrow."

"Um, OK. Hey, can I get another burger? To go?" First rule of negotiation: you can't get what you don't ask for. Besides, the second rule is, what's the worst that could happen? He says no? I can live with that.

"All right."

Yes! I score lunch for Finley, too.

PJ pays for the food. I toss the hamburger bag into the metal newspaper crate strapped to the back of my bike. After PJ pushes open the door to the restaurant with his elbow, he sits on the bench outside of Gina's and crosses his thick legs. Pink knees peek from under his Bermuda shorts.

"You need a ride?" I ask him. It's hot and there's not a smidge of shade. He's gonna bake sitting there in the sun. "Room on the handlebars."

"My driver will be here shortly." He takes a handkerchief from his pocket, pats his forehead, and adds, "Thanks anyway."

A spotless black sedan heads down 5th, glowing like a polished jellybean. Might as well have "PJ" stamped on the license plate. The driver must've been waiting close by for the text from PJ's cell phone.

"See you tomorrow," I holler over my shoulder. Of course he doesn't offer me a ride. He doesn't even turn to wave goodbye.

Just as I'm about to pick up speed 'round the Benton Street curve, the BOGO sign in the window of Eclipse Comic Emporium nearly crashes me into a light post. I got five dollars in my pocket since PJ bought Finley lunch. Buy one comic, get one free? Irresistible. I'll bring home one of his faves and pocket one of my own. It's a win-win day. I don't need a ride home in a big, leather-upholstered, air-conditioned, chauffeured sedan.

The bell jingles my arrival. Selena Kitty saunters from behind a shelf and tries to rub her golden fur onto my legs. I scratch her chin and she rumbles. Her tummy's plump with kittens. Looks like she's gonna drop them any day.

"Afternoon, Mick, what can I do you for?" Mr. Protchensgi peers over an old issue of *Justice League*, his long, graying hair tied back in a tight ponytail today. He stands up straight, and a shark's tooth necklace gleams from a thin rawhide strip at his throat. When he smiles, his two pointy teeth stick farther out than the rest, just like Selena Kitty's, or a vampire. Take your pick.

"Hey, Mr. Gee. Saw your BOGO sign. Is that for everything in the store?"

He chuckles. "Just the new inventory. Classics and vintage are negotiable. As always." He winks.

I don't have the time to bargain with Mr. Gee. He likes to haggle down to the penny, and I've got a burger baking in a basket outside. I flip through the rack marked "New Releases" and grab *Demon Knights* #22 and *Wolverine* #6.

At the counter, Mr. Gee says, "Sale runs all week, you decide to come back." He rings up my total: $4.47. "Better deal than a forty-dollar video game, hey Mick?"

"Sure is." The only time I have forty dollars in my pocket is never.

On the counter display rack is a 1978 issue of *Aquaman* trapped in a net. Batman guest stars, which is a good thing I guess, 'cause he's wearing scuba gear and is rescuing Aquaman. Aquaman gets me thinking about PJ's Sea-Monkeys.

"Mr. Gee, do you know anything about Sea-Monkeys?"

"Sea-Monkeys? You bet I do. Had 'em myself as a kid. Let me see." He digs behind the counter and pulls out a 1979 *Richie Rich*, starts thumbing through the back pages. "Sure to be an ad here somewhere. Yep."

He spreads the magazine on the counter and places his thumb with scary-long nail next to the thick red words: SEA-MONKEYS.

"Own a BOWLFUL OF HAPPINESS! Instant Pets, SO EAGER TO PLEASE THEY CAN EVEN BE TRAINED. Only $1.00."

The hand-drawn picture is lame. A family of red people with webbed feet and hands, lizards' tails, and three-pronged crowns on their heads. The mom has blonde hair and a red bow on her head. There's a pink castle in the background.

"So they're real."

"Real as any other sea creature. Dolphin. Urchin. Mermaid. Octopus."

"Mermaid?"

"Sure. Don't look surprised. Mermaid legends have been with us for centuries. And I always say, every story has a base—"

"Of fact," I finish for him.

Mr. Gee's been telling me and my brother stories as long as we've been coming to his store. He's the one first told me about Zombie Cave and Pirate Pete. Although I haven't the heart to tell him what happened when I visited Pirate Pete myself.

"So have you seen one?" I ask as he hands me my bag.

It will be cool if he has. Maybe he'll tell me where, and me and Finley can track her down. I'd like to meet a mermaid. I wonder if her tail will have a slime coating like a fish. Or if it'll be smooth and dry like snakeskin.

I search Mr. Gee's face. Weather-beaten, sun-leathered, he's spent a lot of time in the water; if anyone's seen one, I bet he has.

"No, sorry. I haven't. But I know who has. Karl Wheetly. He's an ex-Navy Seal. Get him drunk and he'll talk some crazy sea stories. Well, *you* won't get him drunk. Maybe he'll tell you his stories anyway. Last week he's down at the pub raving to anyone who'll listen about a decapitated head he caught in his fishing net.

"Poor Karl, radios the police, says he's bringing the head to shore. But when he docks his boat, all that's left is a skull. Flesh melted into a puddle of goo in the hot sun. Then he goes to pick up the skull and it disintegrates into baby powder in his hands. Police get a plastic bag of sludge scraped from his deck with a film of talc dusted on top. Now there's a story for you."

I nod and smile. Small world. The decapitated head is probably from a two-hundred-year-old pirate zombie I killed, which must've washed out of Zombie Cave when the tide came in. And Karl? He's one of the boatmen who pulled me and Finley out of the surf after we escaped the cave.

"Hope I didn't gross you out," Mr. Gee says. Even though he and I both know he's told me lots worse before.

And, of course, I've seen lots worse.

"Naw. You can tell me anything, Mr. Gee."

"Ha ha." He tap-taps his inch-long fingernails on the counter. "Come back soon, Mick. And bring Finley."

I like Mr. Gee, but jeez, cut the creepy nails already.

Selena Kitty circles through my legs for one last chin scratch, and then I head out the door, fresh comics clutched to my chest.

Outside it's hot enough to make the sidewalk wave at me. The vinyl seat on my bike steams. And

Finley's lunch is gone. Snagged while I spent too much time chatting up Mr. Gee. Maybe the kid who stole it got a big fat bellyache 'cause the burger grew spores in the heat. Yeah. Serves him right.

Make Good on the Deal

"BIG HOUSE." Finley checks out the replica White House PJ calls home.

Big *yard* is going through my mind. "Come on. We gotta use the servants' side."

We both hop off my bike, and I wheel it to a gate around the east side of the house. The latch is unlocked as promised. I hide my bike between a couple of neatly trimmed hedges.

"How do you know him?" Finley almost touches a stone fountain with spouting cherubs but decides to stuff his hands in his shorts pockets instead.

"Booger-Face MacDougal set me up. He's being super nice since we brought back that gold medallion for his dad's museum. I guess it's worth a lot more than the map I ruined."

"That's real good. Wow. Is that a peacock?"

While we're winding up a concrete walkway through a garden of rose bushes, a turquoise body with flowing, vivid tail feathers bobs across our path.

"Yeah."

"Next week we should bring a camera and take a picture for Mom. She'd like to see this."

He's right. Mom's the bird lover in the family. She'd go gaga for the peacock. "We'll have to ask to use the camera first. Looks like the pool is over there."

A couple concrete stairs lead to a scrolled iron gate. The gate is padlocked, but through the ironwork, it's the pool all right. The coolest pool I've ever seen, surrounded by a six-foot, brick wall.

Large trees poke through earth squares in a concrete patio, giving lots of shade on the shallow side. The deep end sparkles in the sunlight like a huge gem. A towering blue slide twists in one corner, and a matching blue diving board rests a few feet off the ground, extending over the water, just begging for my famous cannonball. The circular, in-ground hot tub would look even better filled with suds.

By a striped cabana, a plastic garbage bag with a red baseball cap on top reminds me I got work. "Those must be PJ's clothes. I'm supposed to change into them."

"How you gonna do that?" Finley rattles the gate. "Locked."

"I know, you goof. He must've forgot to unlock it. Guess I'll have to climb." I jam my foot into an opening and scale the scrollwork. Hoisting my leg over the top, I straddle the gate like it's a horse.

"Why don't we ask for the key?" Finley calls up, his eyes wide in his small face.

"It's no big deal. I got this." I swing over the gate and drop to the other side. A shock shoots from my heels through my knees. Nothing I can't handle. Just a reminder that cement is hard. When I stand, Finley's passing through the gate, padlock in one hand, key in the other. He closes the gate behind him with his hip.

"The key was hanging on a peg."

Figures. Rushing versus thinking: the story of me and my brother. Oh well, both ways get us to the other side.

I dash over to the bag of clothes, leaving Finley staring into the deep end of the pool. Hope he isn't freaking out about his swim lesson. It's super important he learn how. For one, we live near the ocean. And two, I've had to save his drowning rumpus twice. So I promised him I'd teach him, and I never go back on my word.

The inside of the cabana is cool and dark. Smells

like sunblock and beach towels fresh from the dryer. I fumble for a light switch by the door, and when I don't find one, I grasp for a string to pull above me. Nothing. Guess I gotta change in the dark.

I bump into a bench. At least I can sit while I switch out my shorts for PJ's and my socks and shoes for his. We are not the same size. He's well-fed, so his clothes hang on me like I'm Stickman. I try to wrangle the belt to cinch it tight and keep his shorts from sagging, but his belt is weird. It doesn't work like a real belt.

Then I figure out it's not a belt. It's suspenders. Yeah, the dork wears suspenders, for stupid, ugly Pete's sake. I think Mom made me wear suspenders for preschool pictures when I was four years old. Thank God no one but Finley is gonna see me.

I exit the cabana.

Finley takes one look at me and squeals like a pig.

Then he snorts.

Then he holds his stomach, bends over, and belly laughs so long and so hard, tears–real tears–stream down his cheeks.

"My own brother." I shake my head, but then I examine myself in the daylight. I am more than an idiot wearing suspenders. Much more.

Pink-and-orange plaid Bermuda shorts, a pink button-down shirt, bright orange suspenders, yellow ankle socks, and black gym shoes, topped off with a red baseball cap. I look like a container of rainbow sherbet exploded on me.

Finley's laughs fill my ears.

"OK, I look like Super Geek. Got it."

"PJ wears this stuff?" Finley hiccups, finally calm enough to look at me without cracking up.

I remember PJ's lunch attire. Tan Bermuda shorts with a baby blue polo shirt, leather sandals. He was preppy, but not a funky, pastel explosion. "He must go all out for yard work."

More incentive for me to mow furiously quick.

"He said the mowers are in the shed south of the pool. Must be that building." I point to the green steel roof I can see just over the brick wall.

"Before you go, you should see what's at the bottom of their pool." Finley points.

I trudge over. My heels slide in the too-big shoes. Blisters in my future for sure. I stare at the bottom of the pool, mesmerized.

Decorated in glass tiles that shimmer and sparkle in the sunlight, a large mosaic mermaid, complete with emerald tail, is embedded in the pool floor. A breeze crosses the surface of the water. The light ripples make the portrait look like it's moving.

"Cool."

"She's pretty."

I pluck a leaf from the jungle of potted plants. "Watch out. She'll hypnotize you. Make you fall in. Kiss you with her cold fish lips." I brush the leaf against the back of Finley's neck.

"Aagh!" He socks me in the arm. "Cut it out."

"Ha. Come on. PJ says you can hang out in the rec room while I mow."

"What's a rec room?"

"Heck if I know. He says it's attached to the garage."

"With the mowers?"

"No. Shed's got the mowers. Garage's got the cars. Come on."

We leave the pool, relocking the padlock behind us, and climb a small, grassy hill to the shed. Note to self, got to mow this hill. From here we can see an expanse of lawn. Great! More grass to cut. And beyond that, an eight-car garage attached to a small house in front of a circular drive that leads to a paved, one-lane road on the property.

"I bet you anything the rec room is that house."

Finley gulps. "I don't want to go by myself. Can't

I help you mow?"

"No. I need to make it look like PJ is doing the mowing by himself. But I'll walk you over."

I jiggle the doorknob. It turns freely so we walk in. That's when I realize REC must stand for Radical Entertainment Center, 'cause PJ's got it all. The house is one room, but it's as big as our apartment. A flat-screen television dominates the back wall. Pool tables, both standard and bumper. Ping-pong table. Pinball machines. Video game consoles, new and old-made-new. Shelves stacked with every board game imaginable, alphabetized. My head is spinning, my stomach's swimming, and the last thing I wanna do is mow the lawn. What's grass?

"What do PJ's parents do, they can afford all this?"

"His mom used to be a supermodel, now she runs a makeup company. His dad is president of some big company outside of town. I don't know what they actually do. Grow money trees."

"Mick? Look at this."

Finley's crouched over a bowl in the center of a round table by a sectional sofa. I put back the gold Wii remote that somehow got into my hand and peer over the lip of the bowl.

Six tiny, red, fuzzy creatures, each the size of a

staple, fan around in the bowl of water. There's also a painted stone castle and two fake plants stuck in some gravel.

"What are they?"

"Don't know." There's a folded note addressed to Finley tucked under the bowl. "This is yours. Read it out loud."

"'Dear Mick's brother Finley. Make yourself at home. I have to suffer through violin and fencing lessons at the big house. Once my teachers leave, then I can show you how some of my toys work. Would you mind feeding my Sea-Monkeys? My dad says he bought more food. It will either be on the snack counter or still in his Bentley. One packet only, please. Thanks, PJ.'" Finley refolds the note. "What's a Bentley?"

"I think it's a foreign car, but I don't know that I'd recognize one by looking at it. Hopefully the food's on the counter."

But it isn't. The only thing on the counter is a dirty plate of half-eaten pizza rolls. When we open the door leading from the rec room to the garage, a series of overhead lights clicks on automatically, bathing us in fake sunshine.

Me and Finley both gasp.

Create Bloodthirsty Mermaid, by Accident of Course

SIX OF THE MOST beautiful cars line up like Christmas ornaments in a box. A cherry-red Corvette convertible with white leather seats. A black Mustang. A silver DeLorean straight out of that old *Back to the Future* movie—one of Mom's favorites she always watches 'cause she likes the actor in it. Those are the three cars I recognize. The other three, I don't know what they are. One of them must be a Bentley.

We walk down the line. A blue car has eagle wings with a B in the center of the hood. Possibly. But there's nothing on the seats inside. There's a car looks like a white Batmobile has two boomerangs for a logo. Maybe. Boomerangs begin with B. On the passenger seat is a silver cylinder with a hinged cap, opened, and a bunch of small, sealed foil packets spilled out. I grab one.

"Got it," I call out to Finley, who's making faces at his reflection in the curve of the third car's fender.

I double-check just to make sure it's not the Bentley. Naw, its logo's got a standing silver lion, paws reaching out. Nothing resembling a B for Bentley and nothing in the front seats.

Back at the bowl, Finley peels open the packet and sprinkles blue powder on the water's surface. The Sea-Monkeys fan to the top, and I imagine they're eating. It's hard to tell 'cause now they're just bait coated in blue sludge.

They don't look anything like the ad Mr. Gee showed me: little merpeople smiling and waving. In reality they look more like brine shrimp, or the stuff whales eat. Krill.

"Weird food. It dyed the water blue."

Finley's right. The water's now deep cobalt. "Must fade after a while. Well, I gotta mow." I give PJ's rec room one more look-see and sigh. "Have fun." Stretching PJ's suspenders into place on my shoulders, I leave for the shed.

I climb on the back of the Williams's mammoth lawnmower. I'm a mowing pro—been doing it around town for spending money since I was nine—so this fancy-schmancy mower's got nothing on me. But there's no wonder PJ's frightened of the machine. It belches black smoke, grinds its blades, and whenever a toad or squirrel dashes out of the way, I swear that lawnmower yanks after the critter. Takes every ounce of my effort to keep the mow lines straight and not chop up wayward wildlife. While gritting my teeth and holding steady to avoid an escaping ground squirrel, I have a crazy thought: I hope the peacock doesn't cross the lawnmower's path.

The Williams's lawn is like a golf course. Except with more shrubbery, buildings, and garden obstacles. So by noon I've switched over to the gas-powered push mower for the detailed work. Sure wish I could take my shirt off. I'm melting out here, but PJ would never be caught without a shirt. I'd spoil our deception if his dad decided to "pop" home early. Of course my head's 'bout ready to "pop" off my neck like a bottle cap. So I soak his clothes in my sweat instead. Glad I don't have to wash them.

PJ did leave me a case of bottled water in the shed. Six are gone. Two down my throat, four over my head. I missed lunch, but honestly, I'm too hot and tired to eat. Hopefully Finley got a snack.

I check my watch when I'm done, done, done: 1:50 p.m., still plenty of time to get that swim lesson in. I hang the trimmer back on its hook, but I don't clean or oil any of the equipment I used. Pretty sure PJ wouldn't know how to do the maintenance. Best to stay in character.

Don't know where I get my last blast of energy, but I sprint to the pool to change back to me. And heck with the key in the padlock, I've got this fence hopping thing down to an art. This time I land like Spiderman. And, yes! This time, no sting in the knees.

When I deliver PJ's sweaty clothes to the rec room, both PJ and Finley are staring into the Sea-Monkey bowl.

"Mick! You've got to see this." Finley dashes over and grabs my arm so hard I drop PJ's clothes.

"Hey."

"Sorry. Come on."

The water in the bowl is clear again, all the blue from this morning either eaten, evaporated, dissolved . . . I don't know where it went, but it's gone. "Wow." Instead of six Sea-Monkeys, there's only one, and it definitely has changed.

Now the size of a man's thumb, it looks like a monkey all right.

A hairy, red monkey with an elongated, scaly fish tail.

Little webby monkey hands.

Little fuzzy monkey ears flattened against its wrinkled monkey head.

A mouthful of razor-sharp monkey teeth.

"What happened to it?" I poke the glass, and the Sea-Monkey bares its teeth at me. Tiny bubbles stream from its mouth to the surface.

"It grew. Quite fast," PJ says. "They all did. And then this one, the biggest, killed the others."

"Where are they now?" There aren't any bodies littering the bottom of the bowl. "Did you pick them out?"

"PJ went to get his fishnet," Finley rushes to say.

"But by the time I got back, this one ... he ... " PJ struggles to continue.

"Ate them. Right up. Tore into them like Rib Sunday at our house."

"Are they supposed to do that?" I ask.

The ad Mr. Gee had showed a happy Sea-Monkey family, not a gang of cannibals.

"No. From what your brother described, you fed my Sea-Monkeys the wrong food, which has ... altered them. You and Finley are responsible for the deaths of my pets and for this ... thing in my Sea-Monkey habitat. You will hear from lawyers. And you will pay." PJ waggles his finger at me.

If Finley wasn't in the room, PJ would be eating my fist. I look at my little brother, and then I breathe before I speak.

"You've got to be kidding me. They're brine shrimp in a bowl. And we followed *your* instructions. There wasn't food in here, so we got it out of the car. The Bentley." PJ is not pinning his Sea-Monkey's personality morph on me and Finley.

"But there is food in here." He prances—yes, I'm using the right word, prances—to the counter, lifts the dirty plate I'd seen earlier, and sweeps a bunch of white packets into his hand. He tosses them on the table in front of me. Sea-Monkey Growth Food. Clearly labeled.

"We didn't see that food," Finley says in a small voice.

"Then let's get the evidence. We'll go to the car and get whatever it is you did feed my pets."

Every time he calls them his pets, I'm torn between erupting in a snort-giggle or twisting his pinky off his hand. A dog is a pet. Certain cats. A nice, fat iguana. Even the peacock he's got roaming his yard. But Sea-Monkeys? They don't qualify as pets.

In the passenger seat of the Bentley, the opened

silver canister is in the same position, silver packets spilled on the brown leather.

"This isn't the Bentley. The Bentley's over there. This is the Citroen." PJ shakes his head. "And why would you think this was Sea-Monkey food?"

It's Finley who stomps his foot. "Why not? Everything here is so rich."

I jump on the bandwagon. "Yeah. Why wouldn't you feed your pets from silver packets that come out of a silver thermos? You have a whole house just for your toys. Your dad has six cars. And they don't look like they get out much."

"They're not meant to be driven. But that's not the point. The point is, you need to go home."

"No."

PJ stares at me, then Finley, then back at me. "I insist you leave. I'll . . . I'll . . . call security."

I am not about to let PJ get away with walking over me, especially in front of my little brother. I stand up straight as I can, even though PJ's a head taller than me today. What? I glance at his shoes. One-inch heels, for Pete's sake. "Yeah? You go right ahead. If you even have security. Didn't see any when I was mowing your lawn for almost five hours." I push my chest into his, my fists clenched. "You owe me and Finley a swim in your pool, and we mean to take it. You can join us, watch us, or sulk with your monkey. Otherwise, I can tell that lawyer of yours about our deal."

His shoulders sag as he stares at the toes of his goofy elevator shoes.

"You're right." He gathers the packets and cylinder from the car. "I'll ask my dad what this stuff is. Show him the Sea-Monkey. Maybe he'll know what's happened to it. Let's get our suits on and swim."

I think PJ just apologized to us.

Agree to Help

"SO HOW'D YOUR FIRST lesson go today?" Mom pulls up a mismatched chair to our kitchen table. Tonight we're having expired food from the grocery store where she has her day job. The bread was a little stale, so she toasted it. The way Mom cooks the chops, they're so tender the meat's falling off the bone. Hard to believe they would've been in the dumpster, but Mr. Wear always lets Mom take some of the expired stuff if she promises to use it that night. The rest gets donated to the wildlife refuge on the edge of town or makes its way to the dump.

"Fine." Finley fills his mouth with pork chop. I know he's avoiding the truth.

Mom knows too, and she fixes her gaze on me.

"For a first day it went fine. He floats good." I grab another piece of toast and smile. "It'll come. You know, the Williams's pool doesn't use chlorine," I change the subject. "They got a copper-silver ionizer. We don't need to use goggles."

She cuts her chop into tiny pieces. She's always been obsessed with keeping me and Finley from choking. I guess it's a habit now. While she's busy at it, she says, "Why do I always get the feeling I'm getting the edited version from you, Mickey?" She chews on one of her chop bits, her fork poised by her face.

"Aw, Mom, you know I don't like Mickey. I'm Mick now."

"You're Mickey on your birth certificate, and you're Mickey to me. Named you for a special reason, and I'm not going back on it now."

"Shoot, Mom. Then just in the apartment, OK?" Anytime Mom calls me Mickey out in the streets, it sets me back months of battles.

"Ha, then don't give me a reason to holler for you."

Finley chuckles and then guzzles his milk. A white mustache frames his lips, and he swipes it with the back of his hand.

"Oh, Uncle George wants you to make a list of items you want him to get for you. He's going to be back in town in two weeks. He says make it challenging. I thought for sure you two stumped him with the unicycle and the miner's hat." She grins. "You have to come up with something really good this time."

Finley and me catch each other's glances. Sea-Monkeys are sure to hit the list. We've got some replacing to do. PJ might have let us off the hook, but the funny thing about guilt is, I can hold my own noose just fine.

Later, Finley and me are settled in our room. More like a closet with a window. He's in the bottom bunk, I'm up top, but I won't be there for long. It's a fact. Warm air rises. And the little oscillating fan Uncle George got us only moves the hot air from one corner to the other. In no time I'm wearing a coat of sweat. I throw my pillow down and jump, and then I stretch out on the rug.

Mom stops in to say goodnight before she walks to the bus stop to get to her third-shift job at the distribution center.

"On the floor again?"

I rise up so she doesn't have to bend so far to kiss my cheek. "Cooler down here."

"Sorry, sweetie, can't get a ceiling fan. See you for breakfast. Love my boys."

"Love you, Mom," me and Finley say together.

I listen for the click of the door locks, but I'm

drifting off quick. The smell of cut grass sinks deep inside my nose. I'll dream of lawn care. And the ceiling fan we can't get 'cause the room's so small the blades would chop me into hamburger while I slept.

Then Finley says all perky, "I had fun today."

Remembering a never-ending hill where the grass keeps growing every time I cut it down, a cannibal Sea-Monkey with razor teeth, and Finley having Zombie Cave flashbacks in the pool during his first swim lesson, I don't agree. But I keep my mouth shut.

"I think PJ could be our new friend. I think he wants to be friends. He has all that stuff and no one to play with."

Now I can't keep my mouth shut. "We can't be PJ's friends. We use the servants' entrance, for Pete's sake."

Finley rolls and parks his back to me. Yeah, he's mad I told the truth, but he needs to hear it from someone. Can't go around thinking he's going to be best buds with Donald Trump and hang out at Disney World all summer.

The phone shrills.

"What now?" I push myself off the floor and trudge to the kitchen. Flick on the light. Squint at the clock on the stove as it flips. 10:14 p.m. My stomach sinks. Only two kinds of calls come after ten. Wrong numbers and trouble. With Mom out . . . "Please be reason one." I pick up. "Hello?"

"Hello? Mick?"

"Yeah."

"It's PJ. I've got trouble."

"So why're you calling me? Where's your Dad? Don't you have . . . people?" No longer worried, now I'm just bugged. "You woke me up."

Finley wanders in, plops in a chair, and starts rubbing his eyes.

"Finley too." I cover the receiver with my hand. "Go back to bed."

"I'm sorry. My Dad never came home. Last-minute overseas business trip. The nanny won't be here until tomorrow morning. My driver is with me. In fact I'm calling from the car. We're outside your apartment building."

I hand the phone to Finley. "Hold this." I part the kitchen curtains enough to peek out. Yep. There under a street lamp in our parking lot, the black sedan standing out like an expensive watch left at the beach.

Grabbing the phone back, I shout, "You're stalking me. I'm gonna call the cops."

"No, wait. Hear me out. I need you to come back to the house. I don't know what to do. With her. I need your help."

"With her?"

"The Sea-Monkey. She's . . . She's not a Sea-Monkey anymore. She's changed again. I can't explain. You have to see for yourself." PJ's voice is squeaky, and it's not the connection.

My curiosity is definitely sparked, but . . . "I can't just leave my place. I got Finley here. Mom's at work. She's hard to get in touch with." And then, because he did drive all the way out here, I offer a deal. "We'll come by in the morning. Look at it then."

"No. It'll be too late." Now he sounds like he's gonna cry. "Please, please. Here. Talk to my driver if you don't believe me."

"What's going on?" Finley asks.

I shrug. "No clue. PJ wants me to talk to his driver now."

"Little Sir. This is the Williams's chauffeur," a bass voice grumbles. "I can drive you out to the house and back. I can also drive to your mother's place of employment and let her know where you are." He pauses, like he's thinking. "In my opinion, the thing ought to be put down."

I can hear PJ protesting in the background, and then he's back in my ear. "So you'll come?"

"Finley's got to come too." I can't believe I'm agreeing to this, but on the other hand, how can I resist? The Sea-Monkey has changed into something an adult thinks should be "put down"? This I gotta see.

"Of course Finley can come."

"Outside in a few." I hang up, and it takes a few seconds to figure what's what. "Get dressed. We're going back to PJ's."

Watch the Mermaid Grow Up

THAT DRIVER BETTER be true to his word. I write Mom a note, just in case. Then I slip back into my shorts and a clean T-shirt, scrunching my feet into my gym shoes.

"We're gonna get in trouble." Finley slips on his flip-flops at the door.

"I'll take the blame for you. I made you come, OK? But you'd better wear sneakers. You never know when you gotta run."

After Finley switches shoes, I lock the door behind us. We walk quietly in the hall so's not to disturb our neighbors, but once we get to the stairwell, we dash down two flights, explode out the door, sprint across the patch of weeds our super calls a courtyard, and finally arrive at the parking lot.

The driver holds the car door open, and we slide across from PJ. The sedan's been customized for four in the back to face each other. PJ's left forearm is wrapped in white gauze and tape.

"What's with the mummy arm?"

"Stitches. Twelve of them. We just came back from the emergency room."

"What happened?" I wonder if PJ decided to give the lawnmower a go.

"The Sea-Monkey. Well, you'll see. She's not a Sea-Monkey anymore."

"Yeah, you said that on the phone, but I thought you were joking. What did it do? Try to eat you?"

"Yes." His eyes glisten in the dark car.

"Wow. Does it hurt?" Finley asks.

"Kind of. I was in shock at first. Now, it feels . . . achy."

I don't know what to say. I stare at PJ's wrapped arm. What could've happened to the brine shrimp since I left that would make it want a piece of PJ? "And what were you doing with your arm in its bowl?" slips out of my mouth.

"Well I wasn't playing with it, if that's what you think. I was moving it to a bigger container." He waves his arm in the air. "I slipped."

That's when PJ's driver pipes up. "The beast latched on tight. I had to hit it with a pool stick to get it to let go."

"Wow," Finley says.

I'm thinking I should've left Finley back home. No wonder PJ's driver wants psycho pet put down.

"By the way, what's your driver's name?" I whisper to PJ. It'd be nice to know what to call the old guy.

"I don't know."

"What do you mean you don't know? How can you not know?"

The clear night sky casts enough light into the car for me to see PJ's face. He doesn't even look guilty. Just shrugs his shoulders.

"Jerkface," I whisper to him nose to nose. "Serves you right, you got bit."

"Mick!" Finley says, but I wave him away.

"Hey, PJ's driver. Thanks for the sweet ride for me and my brother. You got a name so I can thank you proper?"

His dark eyes materialize in the rearview mirror. "Eugene Lazar. You can call me Gene."

"Thanks for the ride, Gene."

"You're welcome."

I cross my arms and try on my smug face. PJ sticks his jaw out and tightens his lips. Finley stares out the window at the almost-full moon while sleeping Beachwood slips by. We ride in our positions the rest of the way.

The main gates open automatically, and the sedan swings around the Williams's ginormous house and down the winding road to the circular drive in front of the garage. We pour out of the sedan and tear to the rec room. While PJ's groping for the key, I hear a strange sequence of sounds through the door.

Growling.

Metallic banging.

Splashing.

Dolphin squeaking.

"Pool sticks are on the wall to your right," Gene says.

"She's scared." PJ turns the knob but doesn't open the door. "We'll go in one at a time. Don't get too close to her." His wild gaze fixes on me. "You want to go in first?"

"Me?"

He nods.

Even Gene's looking at me expectantly.

"Yeah. Yeah." Where's a pitchfork when you need it?

PJ opens the door and stands aside. Overhead tracks blast the space with light. PJ's rec room is a wreck. A pinball machine is crashed wrong side up. The TV's hanging at an angle. Pool balls are scattered on the floor. The area rug's been rolled up. The table in the center is upturned and the fish bowl is gone, replaced with a tin container the size of a small bathtub. A long, red, glossy mermaid tail drapes over the side.

The tail looks like a fake, like PJ hung it there as a joke. I move in closer. Finley's hand presses against the back of my shirt.

The tail twitches.

My feet leave the ground—must be two inches—and the tail flops and bangs against the side of the tub. A webbed, translucent, three-fingered hand with pink claws and hairy knuckles grasps the rim. My breath chirrups against my teeth.

Finley's got my shirt in a sweaty ball at the hollow of my back. The front flattens and sticks against my torso. I can actually see my pulse pounding through the cotton.

I don't want to move in for a closer look, I really don't, but overpowering curiosity's propelling my feet forward, taking Finley with me. This is nothing like a Sea-Monkey.

The veins in the webbing look like roads on a map. Water dribbles off the claws, gleaming under the lights. Three fingers tense and relax, tense and relax. Teasing. Waiting.

I know how this is going to go. Yet still I move in closer, Finley right behind me. PJ and Gene? No idea where they are, and I can't risk looking away from the tub for a second to find out.

Three feet from the creature, a low growl sounds like a pit bull issuing a warning. Pork chops churn in my gut.

"Mick?" Finley whispers.

"Stay here."

But he doesn't release my shirt.

Puddles surround the tub. My feet slide forward inch by inch.

Click, click, click, squeak.

Does the beast want to be a dolphin or a guard dog? I gulp a breath and peer into the tub.

Blinding-white, razor-sharp teeth rip past my forehead. The top of my ear stings. I stumble backward.

Finley slips under me.

Some girl is screaming. There's blood on my shirt. My legs fly out and I slam onto the floor.

Towering out of the tub is a barrel-chested— wearing a bikini top?—gorilla-faced, hairy, red, mermaid monster. Then in an instant, it slips back into the tub with a fierce splash so only its tail is visible hanging back over the edge.

My back's sore. Finley and I are a tangle of legs and arms.

"You two OK?" Gene extends his hand. The other's clamped around a pool stick.

I touch the top of my ear. Sticky. My fingers come back bloody. "Think it nicked my ear."

Finley's shaking next to me. I put my arm around him.

Gene helps us both to our feet.

"She's gotten bigger since we went to the emergency room. We need to move her again." PJ holds up two hangers, each with a cream-colored, padded bodysuit, complete with what looks like oven gloves pinned to the sleeves. "There's helmets, too."

"What are those?"

"Fencing uniforms. We can wear them to protect ourselves when we move her."

He's completely serious. Totally, seriously nuts. I stride to the wall and snap a pool stick from its holder. Gene grips his stick like a baseball bat.

PJ looks at us horror-struck.

I face him calmly. Try to talk to him like I talk to Finley when he's upset. "We need to end this before someone gets hurt bad. This thing is dangerous. If you need to leave while me and Gene take care of business, that's OK. Take Finley with you."

"No." PJ stands between me and the tub, clutching the fencing uniforms. "I won't allow it. She's still my pet. She thinks and feels like you and me, you can't just kill her."

"How do you know? The only thing it's thinking is how tasty we are. What feelings?"

"She's . . . modest."

My eyebrows shoot to the top of my forehead so fast, I feel a breeze under my hair.

He explains, "When we first moved her from the bowl, she lunged for the clothes you wore from mowing. I thought she was going to eat them, or shred them, but she put on the shirt. It must've been uncomfortable 'cause she kept scratching at it, so I threw her one of my sister's swimsuit tops. And you see? She's wearing it. Put it on by herself. A monster doesn't do that. A mermaid does. She's a mermaid. You can't kill her."

"Yeah, was that when she tried to bite your hand off?"

"She just needs more space. A better environment. Please help." He holds up the fencing outfits again. "We're about the same size. Mostly."

I must have a sign that says SUCKER over top my head.

I sigh. "Where we moving her to?"

"The swimming pool."

Move the Mermaid

THE METAL TUB containing psycho fish girl rests inside a large garden wagon. I pull and PJ pushes across the starlit, freshly-mowed lawn.

Lucky for me I'm not claustrophobic. A sieve-type fencing mask restricts my view, cloth covers my neck, and quilted pads hug my chest. I'm a doughboy sweat factory. But at least the couple times Ms. Mermaid's claws have come out, I've been protected.

Finley's gone ahead to unlock the pool gate. Gene's thrown some lengths of plywood over the concrete steps so we can roll the wagon instead of trying to lift it.

In the meantime, our she-devil is thrashing, growling, and generally not making the journey easy. Her tail wallops me across the shoulder, knocking me flat on my back. Again.

Click, click. Squeak.

Honestly, a couple whacks on the noggin with a pool stick could go a long way in taming this beast, but PJ's definitely got a protective streak toward his monkey-turned-monster. I wonder when he's going to tell his dad and if his dad will decide to cut his trip short. After all, his dad's blue powder set the Sea-Monkey down her path to monsterhood.

"PJ? What exactly does your dad do?" I duck as the red tail swings over my head.

"He used to work for the university, doing research. They had a falling out. Pulled his funding. Now he owns and runs his own company. He's quite successful."

"Right. But what does his company do?"

"Genetic engineering."

Genetic engineering? "Um, maybe you oughta put that silver canister in a safe or something. I'd hate to see what'd happen if some mice or ants or flies or something got into those packets." I mean let's be real! Why did PJ's dad go and leave something so dangerous lying around?

"Good idea. After we take care of Marilyn, I'll put the packets and canister in the safe."

Marilyn?

Perched to dump the gorilla fish, now named Marilyn, into the Williams's beautiful pool, I wonder if we're doing the right thing. Finley's swim lessons are getting dumped. No one can use the pool as long as she's living in it. Besides, she could outgrow these boundaries too.

"Ready? One, two, three." We tip the tub off the wagon. The water drains into the pool, but the mermaid's wedged herself in tight. She doesn't budge.

"Pry it out." Gene looms over the tub, pool stick in hand. "Let me help."

PJ lets go of the tub to fend off Gene.

"Hey. Whoa. Guys!" I can't hold the tub myself. It rocks forward, carrying me with it.

Gene drops the stick. He reaches to grab my arm.

The mermaid swipes her tail across his legs.

Me, Gene, mermaid, and tub plunge into the pool.

Claws pierce the flesh on my ankle. I rip off the fencing helmet and swing it, trying to hit Marilyn with it. My shoe lands a sharp kick against something fleshy, and finally I break the surface of the water.

"Swim, Mick. Swim!" Finley shouts.

I'm not far from the edge, but something's happening to the water. It's getting thicker and darker. The glow from the outdoor lights spills in and around the pool, but it doesn't penetrate the water. A gray veil covers the mosaic mermaid. And the mermaid we just dumped has disappeared too. It's like I'm suddenly swimming in watered-down paint, and the fencing suit is a soggy pillow weighing me down.

Gene's head pops up next to mine. He gasps and sputters. Before he catches his breath, he's dragged back under. I struggle to shed the suit, dive under the surface, and search for him, but the water's so murky I can't see him. I can't see a thing. I climb for air.

"Get out of the pool!" Finley's nearly crying.

I can't leave Gene, but I can't help him if I can't see him. And honestly, this water is freaky. Smells, too. Brackish. Like the sea after a horrific storm when the bottom's been churned and thrown up.

PJ hurls a life preserver into the center of the pool. Maybe Gene will see it.

A silver ladder, two feet away, rises out of the pool. I reach for it.

"Marilyn, no!"

A flash of red. An infinitely strong, scaly arm sweeps me under. She grapples me next to her cold, slimy skin. The alien rhythm of her heartbeat pounds through her body and into mine. I can barely see her eyes, gleaming inches from my face. Radiant gold coins. Almost pretty. I could sink into those pools of shimmering light, and that would be OK.

Pain pokes me in the back.

"Ow," I try to say, but my mouth fills with water.

The taste in my mouth and the ouch in my back wake me from whatever trance that sly monster put me under. I slip down instead of up. It's not what she expects, and I slide out of her arms.

With strong kicks I move up and away from her. My arms dig at the surface. I exhale sharply and seize a breath of air. I hope I'll bang into the edge of the pool before she grabs hold of me again.

My hand slaps concrete. Shaking, I pull myself out of the pool.

Finley collapses into me, sobbing.

PJ stands over us holding a telescoping pole.

I rub my back. "Is that what poked me?"

"Lucky I poked anything. Can't see in the pool anymore. I just kept jamming it into the water, hoping you or Gene would find it so we could pull you out." He kneels by me and lets the pole clatter to the ground. "What happened? Where's Gene?"

I gaze at the Williams's swimming pool, now completely filled with squid ink. "Has he come up for air?" There's not even a bubble on the black surface.

"Not since you both went under."

Gene's drowned for sure. Or worse. But I don't say the words. Saying them makes them real.

"What happened down there? You were under so long." PJ hands me a towel out of nowhere.

"Your fishy friend hypnotized me. Then, just when she was moving in for the kill, your poking woke me up and I got away." I wipe my face. The towel gets stained from the blackened water clinging to my skin. Great. My nose hairs are probably dyed black too.

"Marilyn wouldn't kill you. She's probably scared."

"What else do you think she was gonna do to me? Teach me long division?" I have to find something to do before I shake the everlasting sense into PJ. There's a metal box over by the fence. Maybe the pool pump and controls are inside.

"Where you going?" Finley follows me, like he doesn't want me out of his sight.

"We need to drain the pool, find Gene." I don't say "find Gene's body," 'cause I don't want to make Finley more upset than he already is.

"Absolutely not." PJ blocks my path. "You'll murder Marilyn."

My fist scrunches for PJ's first taste of Mick Knuckle Sandwich.

Finley stamps his foot. "Gene can't just disappear. What about his family?"

"He doesn't have family. He lives with us. No one will notice he's gone until my parents come home."

So I punch PJ in the mouth. For Gene. And for me, because even though my hand hurts, I feel better. Course, if I had to do it all over again, I probably wouldn't, mostly 'cause Finley's there.

Tears squeeze out of PJ. The corner of his mouth bleeds. His lip swells before my eyes, but he doesn't lash back. He takes it.

A cell phone chimes from PJ's shorts pocket. He tugs the phone out and checks the caller ID. "Excuthe me," he says around his puffy lip.

"You shouldn't have hit him." Finley can't meet my gaze, and I can't defend myself.

PJ returns with his phone tucked away. "My nanny's here. She'll drive you home. I'll walk you to the gate." He leads us past the pool, still black as a tar pit.

On our way to the front gate, we hear screeching clicks like a mad dolphin from behind us. Goose bumps play leapfrog up my arms.

"I want you to come back tomorrow." PJ looks at his watch. "Today, I mean. Later. During the day. To help me with Marilyn. And to find Gene." He touches my elbow. "Pleathe."

STEP 7

Save the Little Brother, Again

MOM NEVER READS the note I left behind. I tear it up after Nanny Vargas brings Finley and me home, but Mom knows we went to PJ's last night. I don't know how he managed it, but Gene got word to Mom at work, told her where we were and that he would get us home safe. Maybe he called her from the car. I can't bear to tell Mom what really happened.

She's tired and distracted at breakfast. All she says when I tell her we're going back to PJ's is, "He seems like a very needy boy."

"He doesn't have any friends," Finley volunteers.

"Well it's good he has you two." She ruffles Finley's hair and then stifles a yawn. "Don't let him take advantage of you though." She gives me her *protect your brother* look and heads to her bedroom for what little rest she can snatch before going to the grocery store.

I know, Mom.

"Don't forget to clear the table," she calls over her shoulder. The bed creaks, and it's not long before we hear her snoring.

❖ ❖ ❖

It takes forever to get to PJ's. Crossing town on a bike is slow enough, but the sweltering Carolina sun makes carrying Finley more like carrying a two-ton rhino. By the time we pull up to PJ's front gate, the canteen's empty, my legs wobble, and I'm see-through from the ten pounds of sweat I've shed.

"Aren't we supposed to go through the servants' entrance?" Finley tries to shake magically-appearing water drops from the canteen. No luck.

"I'm not a servant today." I press the intercom buzzer and face the camera hanging over the gate. I wave.

The gate rolls inward.

Finley follows as I walk right up to the White House mansion. "We're not going to the rec room?"

"Nope."

A double door looms over us. A huge iron ring hangs from the center of each door. I grab one and try to pound our arrival. It won't budge. I use two hands. The knocker moves an inch.

Finley presses the doorbell.

Nanny Vargas opens the left door. She's a plump, squat woman, and her smile reveals large, crooked teeth polished to a gleaming white. "Boys, good to see you again. Get enough sleep?"

"Yes, ma'am," Finley says.

"Good. Go grab a sandwich from the kitchen and go on out to the pool. Maybe you two can cheer up poor PJ." Nanny Vargas moves aside so me and Finley can scoot inside.

The air conditioning wraps around my hot skin, and man, oh man, I gotta find a restroom now. My gaze darts around the church-sized entryway. "Nanny Vargas? Can I—may I use the—"

She doesn't wait for me to finish. Must notice my legs crossing. "There's a powder room to the left of the stairs."

I dash for it, and my shoes squeak on PJ's varnished wood floor.

The only door to the left of the stairs reveals a restroom bigger than my bedroom. There's two toilets, but one is wonky looking. Got a channel at the front. No lid. I use the one that looks normal.

The hand soap squirts out the beak of a gold bird. Smells like vanilla wafers, which is kinda cool. Towels are stacked inside a gold birdcage, which is kinda whacked. No wonder PJ's odd. He's got no clue how real people live.

When I'm done, Nanny Vargas and Finley are gone from the entryway. I've got no clue how to find the kitchen. I take a few steps and then I realize I'm walking on a giant picture of a peacock with inlaid wood feathers. Definitely a theme going on here.

"Hello." My voice bounces around a bit before getting swallowed by a chandelier draped in . . . yep, crystal birds.

"Over here!" Finley calls out.

"Keep talking so I can find you."

"There's raspberry popsicles and orange soda and watermelon, too."

All of Finley's favorites. Throw in cotton candy and corn dogs, and he's gonna want to get adopted.

I find the kitchen and pretty much decide the Williamses can adopt my whole family, including Uncle George. They've got two refrigerators. Two of everything, really. Well, no, three sinks, if you count the little one by the wood oven.

"Hey cou ohen a hehawhan he." Finley's mouth

is full of sandwich. But since I'm thinking the same thing, I get it: *they could open a restaurant here.*

Nanny Vargas slides a plate stacked high with a sandwich, chips, and a watermelon slice. I dive in. Orange soda fizzes in a towering glass. I wash lunch down and can't help my belch of satisfaction. "S'cuse me."

Nanny Vargas smiles.

Mom would've been all over me.

A cell phone vibrates on the counter. Nanny Vargas pushes a button, picks it up. "PJ?"

"Is Mick here yet?" PJ's talking so loud we can hear him like he's in the kitchen with us.

"Yes, he and his brother are finishing their lunch. Do you want to come up to the house and join them, or do you want them to bring your lunch to you?"

"No. No lunch. You all have to come now. That man you called . . . he . . . fell in. Hurry."

The phone is silent. Finley stares at me, an orange semi-ring of soda staining his face.

"Let's go." I crash off my stool, but I have to wait for Nanny Vargas to lead us out of the house. She winds her way with dainty steps out of the kitchen, through a human-sized terrarium, through a locker room complete with benches, and finally out onto a patio where a golf cart is parked.

I climb in the front seat beside Nanny Vargas. Finley hops in behind me. "You called a guy?" I can't believe I was so sidetracked by PJ's grand house and super sandwiches, I forgot about Marilyn. Deadly Marilyn.

"Yes." Nanny Vargas starts the cart, and we take off over the lawn. She talks while Finley and me hang on tight. She might step lightly, but her driving foot is made of lead. "When I saw how dirty the pool was this morning, I called the pool cleaners right away. They sent a man over before you two arrived. PJ said to wait until his father got home, but with the heat, and you boys coming over, I thought you'd want to go swimming. The water was black, for goodness' sakes."

We pass the Premier Pool Services van parked in the circular drive in front of the garage. The golf cart skids to a halt and I leap out, sprinting up the concrete steps two by two. The gate is unlocked and I barrel through, hoping I'll see a service guy sucking up black ink with his pool vacuum. Gene'll be slapping him on the back. And Marilyn? She'll be nothing but a bad dream.

Instead, there's PJ. Alone. Tears streaking his face,

holding his arms out like he's gonna hug me.

I dodge his grasp. "What happened? Where's the pool guy?"

"He saw Marilyn." PJ wipes at his runny nose with the back of his hand. He stares at the slime on his skin and then at me.

For real. The kid can't even handle his own boogers.

"Use your shirt, dipwad."

"But then my shirt will be dirty."

"Untuck your shirt, wipe, retuck. No one will see. Otherwise they're gonna crust on your hand like wood glue." This is Booger Training 101. Every two-year-old who doesn't have a taste for them has to learn how to properly dispose of them. I almost feel sorry for PJ.

He turns, as if exposing me to such grossness would be improper. Yeah, PJ, I have a few impaled zombie heads I'd like to show you. He finishes business just as Finley and Nanny Vargas reach the pool.

"Where's the service man?" Nanny asks, her gaze darting from lounge chair to lounge chair, not even considering he might still be in the pool. In the water. Under the water.

PJ points to the black surface.

"Oh no. He's . . . ?" Her whole body recoils.

PJ sniffles and then nods.

"Why are we standing around? Call 911! Drain the pool! How do we drain the pool?" Nanny paces, her hands in the air like a football referee signaling a field goal.

"Tell her the truth." I grab PJ's forearm, not about to let him plead out of this one. "Tell her."

He shrinks before my eyes. "I tried to convince the pool man to come back another day. 'Come back next week,' I said." PJ sits on the edge of a pool chair, runs his hand through his hair. What once was blow-dried and sprayed stiff is looking like a greasy hair ball today. "He said, 'I got a job to do,' and he pushed me out of his way. Marilyn didn't like that."

"Who's Marilyn? PJ, where's your phone? Your story can wait, I need to call the police."

"When he bent over to test the water, she pulled him right in. He never came back up." PJ puts his face in his hands.

Finley pats PJ's back like Mom does to us when we're upset. The gesture rolls a stone into my belly. PJ doesn't deserve sympathy. His monster has eaten two grown men. "Enough already."

"Who's Marilyn?"

I don't know if it's 'cause Nanny Vargas keeps asking about her or 'cause I'm yelling at PJ, but darn if that grotesqueness he calls Marilyn doesn't explode out of the pool like a dolphin—splashing ink water everywhere—and then slip back below the bubbly surface.

"Aaaaah!" Nanny screams before she crumples onto a stack of lounge chairs.

Finley rushes to her side and pats her hand. "Mick? Is she OK? She's not moving."

I put two fingers on her neck behind her ear like Uncle George showed me when we were playing combat medic. Her pulse throbs steady through my finger pads. "Must've fainted or something. But she's alive."

Dolphin squeaks and clicks erupt from the pool. Marilyn's broad head and gorilla shoulders pierce the water. Her gold eyes glint in the sun like pirate treasure.

I'm dizzy and grab the back of a pool chair to steady myself. My head is swimming with pirate treasure. Sure wish I could have me a handful of gold coins.

Mom could quit her jobs. We could move into a real house with central air conditioning. I'd have my own bedroom. I'm a real good swimmer, wouldn't take but a couple minutes to swim out, grab those coins from the pool.

"Finley!" PJ's voice cracks.

I rub the sleep from my eyes.

Finley is on the diving board. Walking the plank in a daze.

Marilyn's waiting for him. Scaly arms open wide, claws glistening, teeth bared, eyes . . . no, no, don't look at her tractor-beam eyes.

"Finley!" Both me and PJ are shouting now. If I climb after him, the board will move under my weight. He could lose his balance. The kid still can't swim, and Marilyn's gaping maw salivates.

"Wake up!" I've got to break the spell.

Finley's a couple feet from the board's end. My heart's racing. I grab the closest thing to use as a weapon—a pool chair—and fling it at the monster's head. The chair crashes into the side of her face.

She turns and roars at me.

Finley drops to his knees, gripping the sides of the diving board with his fingers. He inches backward, throwing wild-eyed glances over his shoulder.

PJ coaches him. "You're doing great. Almost there. Don't worry. You got this."

Marilyn screeches, and Finley almost swings his gaze right back to her.

"Don't look at her. Nobody look at her. She's like Medusa. Except instead of turning you into stone, she's gonna drown you and eat you." I don't mean to give my little brother more nightmares than he already gets, but if what I say saves his life, a few nightmares are worth it.

When Finley gets off that diving board, I hug him. Hard.

"Ouch."

Maybe too hard. "Thought I was gonna lose you, buddy." I hug him again, softer.

Marilyn starts her dolphin calls again.

I have to pretend I've got someone holding my head straight toward PJ and Finley. "Jeez. We need something to keep from looking at her."

"Do you think super-dark sunglasses will work? I've got a box with different sizes in the cabana." PJ points to the striped tent where I changed into his clothes yesterday. "We could try them out."

"Yeah, sure, if you're the guinea pig who's gonna look into her eyes with them on." I lead the way, Finley on my heels, PJ close behind.

Marilyn splashes and growls.

Feed the Mermaid

INSIDE THE CABANA, PJ digs inside a tub molded to look like a pirate's chest. He pulls out a box filled with rows of plastic-wrapped sunglasses. "Pick one."

I pluck out two pairs and hand one to Finley. "How come you got so many?"

"Guests are always losing theirs. We like to make sure they're comfortable."

"You got a box of wallets, too?"

PJ's about to say something back to my snarky comment when a giant splash draws our attention.

We sprint outside. I'm pushing the too-big glasses up the bridge of my nose. Finley's pulling his out from his ears 'cause they're clamped around his face too tight.

Marilyn's back underwater so we don't even get to try them out. A series of concentric circles are rippling underneath the diving board. They get wider at the edge of the pool like the wake from a boat. A chill scoots down my spine. I've seen these kinda waves in pools before. Right after someone does a cannonball.

I scan the stack of lounge chairs where we left Nanny passed out.

She's gone.

"Argh." My blood boils. I start flinging chairs into the pool. "You crazy monster." A chair smashes the diving board with a clatter, sinks into the black water. "Stop eating everyone!" I whip one over my head. It splashes dead center. "What's wrong with you? They're people. Sea-Monkeys don't eat people. Argh." Another chair shakes in my hands.

"Maybe if we feed her something else." Finley touches my arm.

I can't see his eyes through the dark sunglasses squeezing his face, but his voice sounds choked. I set the chair down.

"That's a great idea." PJ prances over to us.

I'm thinking he's due for another punch in the mouth, but instead I sit in the chair, clasp one hand over my fist. Not in front of Finley.

"Let's go to the house and see what we can find." PJ's already at the gate.

I don't move. "You go. Finley and me can . . . watch the pool." Call the cops. Kill this bloodthirsty monster snacking on grown-ups.

PJ may be stupid in love with his pet, but he's not stupid. "No. Finley can stay if he wants, but I don't trust you alone with Marilyn. You might've hurt her with those chairs. I don't want you to do any more damage."

"I'm not leaving Finley alone with her."

"Then we'll all go."

PJ drives the golf cart back to the house. He's not a speed demon like Nanny Vargas, so it takes us twice as long. On the way, Finley asks, "Do you think Nanny's really in the pool? Maybe she left to get help?"

"Maybe," I tell him. But I don't believe it for a second. She would've called out for us. She wouldn't just leave. No. I know what happened. She woke up, got hypnotized, and jumped into the pool. Of course I'm not telling Finley.

PJ inches the golf cart up to the patio and turns off the engine, but instead of leaving the keys in the starter, he takes them with him. What's he think, I'm gonna sneak back and off Marilyn while he's not looking?

I actually didn't get the idea until he took the stupid keys.

We don't go back into the kitchen. PJ takes us into

a room he calls the pantry. I call it PJ's convenience store without the cash register. Smells good. Soup mix, salami, Doritos.

PJ tears off a black plastic garbage bag from a roll on a spindle. "Let's try the cans over there."

Packed on a shelf are cans of tuna, crab, shrimp, chicken, and SPAM.

"You eat SPAM?"

"My dad. He likes greasy foods. Especially pizza rolls. Let's take it all."

We end up dividing the cans into two bags to spread the weight. Finley and me each have a bag in our lap on the way back. I've got the can opener in my shorts pocket. For some reason, PJ insisted I grab a spoon, too.

If he tries to feed Marilyn like a baby, I will barf on them both.

At the edge of the pool, the three of us lower our sunglasses back over our eyes. I've got three cans of tuna, one can of crab, and a can of SPAM open when Marilyn emerges.

"Should we float the cans out to her? Like boats?" PJ asks.

What a goof. "They'll sink. She can come and get them."

PJ grabs the spoon and a can of tuna. He scoops a chunk of fish and puts it in his mouth. "Look Marilyn. It's food." He chews. Swallows. "Yummy." He sets the can and the spoon back down with the rest.

He's a dork with his exaggerated movements and high-pitched baby talk. But she slices through the water to the side of the pool, her gaze fixated on those cans.

I back up. Hold my breath.

One claw pokes the tuna. She tilts her head. Nostrils flare and sniff. A grumble bellows from her throat. With the side of her index finger, she digs a ridge of tuna into her mouth. Then she slams the can to her face, and after a couple slurps, she crushes the empty can and throws the metal ball at PJ's feet.

The canned food gets devoured in an assembly line. Marilyn freaks when she tastes SPAM. She spins. She licks her fingers all the way up to her hairy knuckles. She belches. And instead of crushing the can, she holds it to her chest, squeaks, and then disappears with it below the water.

"She likes the SPAM." Finley retrieves more SPAM cans from his plastic bag.

They have pop-tops, so I don't need the can opener for them. We alternate the SPAM with every eight or nine cans of other stuff 'cause we don't have enough.

She doesn't slow down for a second. Keeps eating and eating. Although she must be hoarding SPAM cans, 'cause she drags them underwater and they never reappear. The other cans are crushed and tossed, forming an interesting modern art teepee.

My wrist hurts from turning the crank on the opener. I cut myself on the edge of a shrimp can lid. A bit of my blood drops into the meat.

PJ sets it at the edge of the pool with the others.

"Whoa, wait!" I don't want that monster to get a taste of me. I reach for the can.

Marilyn gets there first. She holds the can and sniffs. Her nose scrunches, and then she hurls the can over the brick wall. Sounds like it hits the golf cart.

"I don't think she likes you." PJ replaces the shrimp with a can of SPAM, and Marilyn coos.

"I don't like her either." Her not liking my blood doesn't sit right with me. I don't care if she doesn't like me, but blood is blood, and she's a bloodthirsty monster.

We're about out of cans. Two left: chicken and the last SPAM. But Marilyn doesn't seem to be slowing down. When she finishes, she lets out a belch even Larry Zuckowski from school couldn't match after a liter of pop.

She scans our faces. The sunglasses must be working, or she hasn't turned on her tractor-beam eyes, 'cause I have no desire to take a swim. Instead, Marilyn lets loose a high-pitched squeal so intense I drop to my knees. It's like a harpoon piercing my brain.

Finley clutches his ears. PJ curls on the ground. Then every light around the pool shatters. Glass flies like crystal birds.

Marilyn slips below the surface of the water, leaving the three of us surrounded by a blanket of shards. "Jingle Bells" rings inside my head.

"What was that?" Finley uncovers his ears.

PJ sits up and shakes glass from his shirt.

I stand. My shoes crunch when I move my feet. "Either she's mad her feast is over, or she just said, 'Thanks for lunch, when's dinner?'"

Formulate a Plan

PJ WHIPS OUT his cell phone. "Beachwood, North Carolina. Sunview Market on North Main, please."

"What are you doing?" I don't know why I'm whispering. Maybe I don't wanna draw Marilyn and her ravenous appetite above the surface. "How do you know the grocery store my mom works at?" I hope she doesn't answer PJ's call. She'll recognize his name. Interrogate me as soon as she sees me. *What were you kids up to, Mickey?*

"It's the store Nanny Vargas orders from all the time. The name's on the bags brought into the house." PJ stares at the phone, waiting.

"Sunview Market found. Would you like to be connected?" The voice coming from his phone sounds like a sleepy robot lady.

"Wow. He's got a smartphone." Finley tries to look over PJ's shoulder.

PJ starts talking to the phone again. "Yes, connect me." He realizes Finley and me are hovering and switches off the speaker, putting the phone up to his ear. "Hi. I want to order some groceries for delivery . . . No, can you look it up? The Williams's account. I'm PJ Williams . . . As soon as possible . . . If I have to." PJ looks over at me. "They're checking."

"Checking for what?"

"Hang on, she's back. Yes, I'm still here . . . Uh huh . . . we need cans of tuna, shrimp, crab, and–"

"SPAM!" Finley shouts like he's sharing his Christmas wish list, with Santa, during a blizzard. "Don't forget the SPAM!"

"And SPAM . . . How much? Well, what've you got? . . . OK . . . Yes, all of it . . . Fine, call them, but they put my name on the account so I could get whatever I want whenever I want it . . . I'm just telling you they won't like being interrupted by a call from you. They don't even want me to call unless it's an emergency." PJ starts pacing.

I keep my mouth shut. If PJ needs an emergency to call his parents, a killer mermaid in his swimming pool should qualify. I don't want to know what he thinks is an actual emergency.

"Good. So when can we expect delivery? . . . Super . . . Oh, wait. Do you have any fresh fish? . . . Too bad." He slips his phone back in his shorts.

"Well?" I don't hassle him for using the word "super." I must be getting used to his hoity-toity talk. As long as I don't start using words like "super" and "pop on over." Kids in my part of town would bust me in the chops.

"Delivery truck will be here in an hour. They're bringing at least fifty cans of each thing. We can feed Marilyn for days."

My gaze wraps around the pyramid of crumpled cans. "Not likely." She'll have her new stash devoured by tomorrow.

I flex my fingers. They're stiff from opening all those cans. Red dents decorate my palms. Flipping my hands in front of PJ's face, I say, "Who's gonna open them this time?" The slash from where I cut my finger practically glows.

"The electric opener. We'll open the cans in the kitchen, stack the open cans in a box, and then bring the box out to her."

"It's a good idea. Don't you think so?" Finley sounds like he's trying to force PJ and me into buddying up. He doesn't know better.

"You know you've got to keep the delivery man away from the pool, or Marilyn will snack on him too." When I say her name aloud, I check the pool for ripples. I know she listens. Waiting to pounce.

I'm about to ask PJ how long he expects to keep this up. The town will run out of canned seafood before his parents get home. He's blabbing away about grocery store accounts, and I'm wondering, what about his parents? He's gonna have to spill about his pool pet eventually.

But PJ distracts me when he says, "Karl Wheetly."

"What did you say?"

PJ thumps his forehead with the heel of his hand. "Pay attention already. I said the grocery store ran out of fresh fish. Fresh food could fill Marilyn up better than the canned stuff. The grocery clerk said lots of locals went fishing this morning. She said one of the fishermen always supplies the store. He might have some. His name is Karl Wheetly."

"That's it!"

Finley takes a step back and nearly crashes into the stack of cans.

I grab his hand quick and pull him back to standing. "Sorry, bud." Who knows what crazy Marilyn would do to him if he knocked down her tower. Flop out of the pool after him. Chomp him from the ankles up.

"What's *it*?" Finley gets his balance.

"Karl Wheetly. Mr. Gee told me when I bought the

comics that Karl Wheetly's seen a mermaid before. He's the one adult that won't freak if we tell him about Marilyn. Maybe after talking to him, we'll know what to do with her." I slap my leg. "And he knows me. Pulled me and Finley out of the ocean last month."

"I don't know. What if he wants to capture her and put her in a zoo? Adults never understand."

I don't tell him most kids won't understand his attachment to a people-eating, monkey fish either. And how he seems to care more about Marilyn than his own nanny.

"Look, I'll go talk to him. I'll ask about getting my hands on his catch of the day first, hint around about mermaids, and hear what he's got to say."

"Don't give him details. I don't want him coming after Marilyn with nets and a harpoon."

Nets and a harpoon? Not a bad idea.

My eyes must flash or something, 'cause PJ grabs Finley's wrist. "Your brother stays while you go. And I won't let you back through the gates unless you're alone. Without weapons."

PJ hasn't gotten it through his thick head. No one threatens to keep the Bogerman brothers apart. No. One. I try on my calm voice even though I want to shot put PJ into the pool. "Let go of my brother. Now."

He hesitates.

I clench my fingers into a ball.

PJ loosens his grip.

Finley slips his wrist from PJ's grasp. "I want to stay. You can go faster on your bike without me."

I shake my head. "What if PJ decides to feed you to Marilyn while I'm gone? I can't protect you if you stay with him."

"I would never let anything happen to him."

"You don't get a say." I give PJ my X-Men-laser-burn-through-your-brain stare.

"Why can't you believe I can take care of myself? Remember the cave?"

Of course I remember Zombie Cave. The worst of the memories still catch me in my sleep. "But you can't swim."

"I'm not gonna need to. I have sunglasses now so she can't sneaky-eyes me into the pool." Finley stands tall. Sticks his chin out. "I'll be OK."

PJ stays quiet while I think a minute. I know how my brother feels, wanting to prove himself. I get it.

"OK." I glare at PJ. "But I get to take one of your cell phones so I can talk to my brother whenever I want."

"There's one in the kitchen. Nanny left it," Finley says.

Already I'm a little better with leaving Finley. He notices things. Like the phone. And he can be real smart sometimes.

"Let's go back to the house. Finley and I can wait for the delivery. You can take the phone and bike out to the docks. We'll check in with each other every hour."

"Half hour."

"OK. Half hour."

"And Finley and me need to call our mom at work to let her know we're staying." She'll probably be relieved when we ask to spend the night. One less meal she'll have to scrape together. Payday isn't until next week.

We leave Marilyn and her inky-black lair behind.

"I want to drive the golf cart this time." Finley stakes his claim in the driver's seat. The keys are still in the ignition.

PJ smiles and climbs in the back.

I plop into the seat next to Finley. "OK, show us what you can do."

As the golf cart hiccups across the lawn, Marilyn's dolphin calls follow on the breeze.

Meet a Fisherman

THE DOCKS ARE SOUTH of the marina, past Cutter's Crag. By the time I get there, the sun is already starting to drop. I'll have to bike back in the dark. At least my bike is plastered with reflectors, and the moon will be full tonight. It should be bright enough to light my way.

Fishermen buzz around on the worn wood pier, tying off their boats for the day, lugging their catch to their trucks, hailing and howdy-do-ing each other. A cloud of fish stink hovers above everyone and everything. There's a wet dog sticking his snout in a bucket of minnows. When I walk past, he doesn't smell like wet dog. Yep, he smells like fish.

Eddy Rubin from The Seafood House has his trailer and buys flounder on the spot, probably for tonight's special. He makes a mean fish stew. Mom splurged and got a big container for me when I had pneumonia last year. Or, as I like to say, the month an invisible elephant sat on my chest.

I wave, and Mr. Rubin salutes me then goes back to negotiating for a cooler full of blue crab. I scan faces for a guy who looks like he stepped off a box of frozen fish sticks.

Karl Wheetly raises his head above a stack of crates. His salt-and-pepper beard glistens in the fading light.

"Mr. Wheetly," I call out and weave my way over to him. "Do you remember me?"

His lips purse. He scratches his head.

"You pulled me and my brother outta the water near Cutter's Crag last month."

He ruffles my hair. "Yes. Hardly recognize you when you're not sopping wet." He extends his other hand and I shake it. His calloused palm is sandpaper against mine. "Staying out of trouble?"

I avoid the question. "Can I buy some of your fish?" I finger the fifty-dollar bill PJ gave me, now stashed inside my pocket. I swear it's warm, like all that money really is gonna burn a hole in my pocket.

"You here with your parents? How you getting the fish home?" Mr. Wheetly's gaze traces a path behind me to the parking lot.

"No, just me." My bike's propped against a piling. I point. "Brought my bike. I can carry a lot in the basket."

"OK then. I can fix you up with a few redfish. Someone on your end knows how to scale and grill them?"

Marilyn will probably choke them down her gullet whole, but I say, "My mom's done it before."

"Pull up your bike."

I wheel through the crowd, careful not to pick up a stray hook in one of my tires. Mr. Wheetly's got five huge redfish on a bench. "Look OK to you?"

"They're great. How much?"

"Five bucks a piece?"

"Wow. Are you sure? I can pay more."

"They jumped into the boat. They must want to be served up with lemon and tartar. Who am I to deny them their heart's desire?" He wraps each fish in newspaper and tapes the packets closed with a strip of packing tape. Then he wraps the packets into one larger newspaper bundle and tapes it shut.

I hand him PJ's fifty-dollar bill. Sure wish I had some cash of my own. Mom would love to fry up one of these beauties for po'boy sandwiches.

"Gotta make change." Mr. Wheetly strides over to his boat, The Isabella. In one swift stretch, he hops on board and disappears below deck.

I lower the fish bundle in my basket and figure

it's about time to give Finley a call.

He answers on the third ring. "Hey, Mick. You OK?" Sounds like a semitruck is squealing to a stop in the background.

"Yeah. And you?"

"Yeah," he shouts. "We're bringing dinner out to Marilyn."

My stomach flips. "Wait till I get back. I just bought some fish."

"She's been screeching. She can't wait. PJ says we gotta feed her right now. She's so loud, he's worried someone driving by the house will hear her."

My stomach flops. "Let PJ feed her. Don't get close to the pool. Got it?"

"Jeez. I got it. I'm fine, OK?"

"Let's keep it that way."

"Trouble?" Mr. Wheetly's next to me with a twenty and a five in his upturned palm.

"Gotta go," I say into the phone and press end.

My heart wants me to snatch the change, jump on my bike, and speed outta here. Imagining Finley near Marilyn when she's in feasting mode makes the hairs on my arms turn into porcupine spines.

My head knows that now I've got Mr. Wheetly's attention, I need to ask my questions. It's my chance to come up with an overall Marilyn solution.

"No trouble." I take the bills. "But—" That's not a word I like hanging in the air, except it hangs there until Mr. Wheetly breaks the spell.

"But what? Something on your mind?"

Here goes. I breathe in deep to reinforce my nerves and nearly cough on the smell. "I need to talk to you about mermaids."

Mr. Wheetly coughs instead.

"Mermaids," he says once he recovers. "And what makes you think I know anything about mermaids?"

"People in town." I don't give Mr. Gee away. He's a friend.

Mr. Wheetly glances over his shoulder. His voice drops so low, I gotta strain to hear him. "How 'bout we put your bike and your haul of fish in the back of my truck? We can talk while I drive you home."

That could work if I wanted to go home. And showing up with Karl Wheetly at PJ's door breaks my promise. No adults near the mermaid. She likes to snack on them. Plus, this adult smells like fish. It'd be dangling a human-sized mouse in front of a tiger.

"My mom will get mad if I take a ride from someone she doesn't know. House rules." Shoot, that even sounds like a rule she'd make.

"You must not have told her about your rescue ride in my boat then." He raises an eyebrow, cracking his forehead into ridges.

Caught. "No." I stare at my shoes. "Will you still tell me about mermaids?"

"Tell you what, why don't I buy you and me a drink—some coffee—at Cuppa Café, up the hill. You ride your bike, and I'll follow in my truck." He pokes the fish in my basket. "I have a cooler in the cab. Best we put these on ice while we talk."

Cuppa Café has only three people inside when we get there. Two silver-haired ladies sit at the counter picking at pie slices. One wears a sun hat, even though the sun set. Looks like a flying saucer landed on her head.

A young guy in an apron wipes off tables. He raises his head when he hears us. "Fresh pecan pie and lemon squares tonight. Can I get you some?"

"Two coffees. Two lemon squares." Mr. Wheetly pulls out a chair for me and then takes one for himself.

I've never had coffee. It's cool Mr. Wheetly thinks I'm old enough to drink it. When I try it, I think adults must have worn out their taste buds. Stuff is bitter nasty, like chewing tobacco, which I also tried once and almost puked, except this stuff is uber hot. Makes it ten times worse. I dive into the lemon square instead. Now if they could make a drink from this, I'd be on it like that alligator on Mrs. Toler's poodle last spring.

"Good, huh?" With one bite, Mr. Wheetly clips his lemon bar in half. He makes the same sugar-rush smile Finley makes after he's eaten a row of cookies from the pack. He swallows. "Usually this place is crowded. Lots of folks must be at the pavilion tonight. Ethan Blanco's performing. You going?"

"No." I lick powdered sugar off my fingers. Ethan Blanco plays boring new-wave jazz on a saxophone. Even if I weren't trying to save the world, I wouldn't go see Ethan Blanco.

"All righty. Enough small talk. Why so interested in mermaids?"

My brother's looking after one that lives in a swimming pool. A kid I know named it Marilyn. I've seen it drown three people. It's tried to kill me a couple of times. "Just interested," I say.

"Well it's best not to be too interested. Mermaids have a bad reputation for a reason." Mr. Wheetly sips his coffee.

"I didn't know they had a bad reputation. I thought they were supposed to be sparkly and pretty and sing or something." The girls in school sketch mermaids on their notebooks, watch mermaid cartoons after school, and dress like mermaids on Halloween.

"That's in the movies. In the real world, they draw sailors to their deaths on the rocks. Men, lured by the mermaid's song, will plunge into the sea, swim into their cold, dark embrace, and drown."

"Women too," I blurt, remembering Nanny Vargas.

"Aye. Women too. Legends say the mermaid covets all human lives: men, women, children. I barely escaped, myself."

"Really? What happened?"

Mr. Wheetly suddenly ages twenty years. His sun-burned cheeks turn ash-colored. "First time I saw her near Montez Cove. About ten years ago. I thought she was a woman washed up on the rocks, clinging for life. I brought my boat around, hoping to help, but I couldn't get close. The sea was angry. Storm racing down the horizon. I shouted to her, and she slipped beneath the waves. The tail? A trick of the light."

"You saw her tail?"

"I didn't believe I saw her tail. Not then, anyway. What I thought I saw was a woman who died before my eyes. I went to the beach every day for a couple of weeks, sure her body would wash up. Then I thought the sharks must've gotten to her."

Adults always blame the sharks.

The waiter refills Mr. Wheetly's cup. Mine is still full, and he has to yank the pot up before he pours and overflows. When the waiter returns to the counter, Mr. Wheetly picks up where we left off.

"Then I went to the beach at night. She was there. Treading water a few yards beyond the whitecaps. Caught her face in my flashlight. Her eyes sparkled like jewels. I called to her, and this time she sang back to me."

"What were the words?" I interrupt.

"I don't remember. All I know is, her voice stirred my soul. All I wanted was to be with her. Nothing else mattered. I ripped off my shoes, tore off my shirt, and swam out after her." He drinks a long swig of coffee and stares past me over the rim of his cup.

"Well she didn't drown you. You're here."

"No. I didn't drown. She left before I could get to her. But the point is, I wanted her to take me. To hold me and pull me under. I swam for an hour looking for her, and when I couldn't swim anymore, I went and got my boat. Putted around the cove looking for her all night, and every night after for an entire summer. Even now, sometimes I go and look. Especially if it's a night like tonight."

"What's special about tonight?"

"Full moon."

Mr. Wheetly doesn't explain, like he thinks I already know why a full moon is important. But I don't get it. Maybe he has improved vision in the moonlight. That'd make sense. "You can see her better?"

"During a full moon, mermaids get their legs."

STEP 11

Try Not to Panic

I PICK THE BOTTOM OF MY JAW off my chest. "Legs?"

"Sure." Mr. Wheetly stuffs the second half of the lemon square in his mouth and swallows without chewing. Reminds me of Marilyn scarfing down tuna and SPAM. I wonder how many gulps it took her to eat Gene. If she sprouts legs and starts sprinting around town, with her appetite, no one will be safe.

"I gotta go, Mr. Wheetly. Need to get that fish back. People are, um, Mom is expecting me."

"You OK? You're looking a little green around the gills."

"Ha, fisherman-speak. I'm fine. Just thinking of the trouble there will be if I'm too late." I push away from the table. "Thanks for the dessert." I cross the café in a couple strides.

"See ya 'round, Mick," Mr. Wheetly says to my back, 'cause I'm out the door and calling Finley faster than you can say Psychotic Monster with Legs.

My heart does a flop into my belly. The ringing goes on and on. "Pick up. Come on, pick up." I get nothing. When it switches to PJ's voice mail, I end the call.

Tucking the phone away, I skid my bike over to Mr. Wheetly's truck to retrieve the fish. His cooler's in the bed, so I have to climb over the tailgate. No problem. I grab the bundle. Heave ho over the side.

My pocket chimes. Whoa! I crash and crush the front wheel of my bike. Both of us flattened on the parking lot's asphalt. I struggle to pull the phone out from under me.

"Hello?"

"Margarite Vargas, please," a woman's voice says.

"Who's this?"

"Lara Williams. Who's this? And why do you have Margarite Vargas's phone?"

It's PJ's mother. Oly moly. The thinking-fast part of my brain just hopped a bus to Canada. "Um. This is PJ's friend, Mick. How're you doing today, Mrs. Williams?"

"Where's Nanny Vargas?"

"Um . . . she . . . um . . ." At the bottom of your pool. "She's in the restroom."

"Well you shouldn't answer someone else's phone. Adult calls are private business. Next time, you let it go to voice mail. And you shouldn't reveal when someone's in the restroom. That's private business too. You should say Nanny Vargas is indisposed and she'll have to return my call."

"Indisposed." Now I know where PJ gets his fancy talk. And Nanny Vargas is definitely indisposed. Yessiree.

"Put PJ on the phone. He isn't answering his."

"Um . . . he . . . um . . ." Could also be at the bottom of your pool. "He is indisposed and he'll have to return your call."

"He's in the restroom too?"

I don't get why she talks in code if she's gonna break the code seconds after she makes the code. "Yes. But a different restroom. They're not in the same one."

"Oh all right. Please have them both call me when they're available. And, Mick?"

"Yes, ma'am."

"You wouldn't happen to know why over six hundred dollars of canned goods were delivered to the house today?"

"Um . . . they . . . um . . . no, ma'am."

"Never mind. Just have them call me." She clicks off.

For someone teaching me phone manners, it's kinda rude she didn't say goodbye. But the shorter the conversation with PJ's mother, the better. I need to get back to PJ's quick. If he's not answering his mom's calls either, he might really be at the bottom of the pool with Marilyn.

I have to see my brother.

I stuff the fish into my bike basket, hop on, and start pedaling. The front wheel wobbles. I can't pick up the pace. The wheel must've bent when I crash-landed. I can only manage half-speed 'cause the tire's rubbing the frame.

"Ugh! A break, all I ask is to catch a break."

The phone chimes in my pocket. If it's PJ's dad, I doubt if telling him everyone is indisposed is gonna hold him off. This time I check who's calling before I answer. It's PJ.

I let him have it. "How come you haven't been answering your phone? Is Finley OK? You need to call your mom. She's trying to teach me manners and asking questions about Nanny Vargas and food from the grocery store and—"

"Stop talking!" PJ yells.

I clamp my lips and listen. There's a steady engine patter in the background. Sounds like he's riding in the golf cart.

"Now don't freak out." His tone says freak out now.

"What is it?" He's going to tell me Marilyn grew legs. I know it.

"Just shush and listen, OK? Everything was fine. Marilyn settled down after dinner. She dived under the water nice and quiet. Finley and I were sitting around the pool talking. It was good."

If PJ drags this out any longer, I'm gonna reach through the phone and sock him in the nose.

"But then something happened."

"Ahh—get to the point."

"Marilyn. She climbed out of the pool. Right up the ladder. She has—"

"Legs."

"How'd you know?"

Usually I like being right. Not this time. "Full moon."

"Yeah. There is a full moon. Gosh, I didn't even think of that. It's really bright, too. Lights the place up. But that's not all. There's more. She doesn't just walk now."

I can't even imagine what else she can do. Shoot lasers out of her golden eyeballs? Spit acid?

Breathe fire?

"She talks."

Now that, I didn't expect. "What'd she say?"

"More food."

Figures. "Put Finley on the phone. I want to talk to him now." Once I hear Finley's voice, I'll be able to think straight.

"He's not here."

"So where is he?" I grip a handlebar with my free hand, steadying my bike, steadying me. If PJ tells me Finley's indisposed, I'll crack.

"He's with Marilyn."

Track Down the Mermaid

I CAN'T BREATHE. PJ force-fed me a boulder, and now it's pressing on my lungs from the inside. Rock hard and solid.

"Mick? You still there?"

Air squeezes past my lips in a squeak.

"It's OK. Really. Finley wanted to go with her. It's like he volunteered."

My breath comes back in a scream and I set off a grapevine of dog barks around town. If the street weren't empty, traffic would stop. Luckily, no one pokes their head out a window. "He volunteered to be *more food*? Are you crazy?"

"No, no. Calm down. I told her we could order more from the grocery store, and she said, 'Noooo. Nooooww.' Then Finley said, 'We can go to the grocery store ourselves.' So Marilyn scooped him up and ran out the gate with him. You should see how she runs. I tried to catch up with them, but

I lost them pretty quick. Now I've got the golf cart so I can go faster."

Crumpling to my knees, I let my bike fall in the street. "She's going to eat him." My tears spill before I can squeeze them back.

"No, no. If she wanted to eat him, she would've done it by the pool. She could've eaten both of us if she wanted. And when she carried him off, he wasn't hollering for her to let him go. He didn't fight at all."

I let PJ's words sink in. OK, Marilyn didn't eat Finley at the pool. Maybe Marilyn snatched Finley for insurance. In case she doesn't find anything else worth eating, she can eat him later. "Where do you think they went? I gotta get him back."

"Well I've been following their trail while we've been talking. She's got slimy footprints. They're silver in the moonlight. Easy to follow, like a snail's path. Lucky for us, huh?"

My first instinct is to take off and search for silver footprints. My second instinct is to find PJ and pummel him into a slimy puddle for not watching out for Finley. "Where are they going? Where are you?"

"I'm a couple blocks south of Sunview Market. I think that's where they went. Good thing Marilyn's wearing Nanny Vargas's skirt. That would've been embarrassing if she ran into the store without anything on her bottom. Does Finley have any money on him?"

"Money? Who cares about money? I'll meet you at Sunview. And, PJ . . . if anything happens to my brother–if he gets even a stubbed toe from this–I will personally stuff you inside Zombie Cave. Forever. Got it?"

"I think Marilyn likes him. He'll be fine," PJ says, but to me it sounds like he's trying to convince himself. The quiver in his voice before he clicks off is a dead giveaway.

I'm at least a mile east of the store, and my bike is useless for getting anywhere fast. I kick the wheel frame to get the bend out and make the bend worse. I'll be faster on foot. I ditch my bike in an alley, grabbing the fish packet before I sprint up Breaker Street.

Maybe I can use the fish to lure Marilyn away from my brother. Hopefully raw fish tempts her even though she's been eating the cooked, canned kind.

My shoes pound and scrape when I run. I use the beat to distract my thoughts from Finley. Pound, scrape, pound. *Mom could've cooked this fish up nice.*

My lungs start to ache. Pound, pound, scrape. *Mom's a great cook when she has the time*. My calves burn. *When she isn't working at the distribution center*. Pound, pound. My left thigh starts to cramp. *Or the grocery store*.

Oh no.

Marilyn might not have a taste for Finley, but she's proven she can gorge on more than one adult per day: Gene, Pool Guy, Nanny Vargas.

Mom.

❖ ❖ ❖

When I get to the grocery store, PJ tumbles out of the golf cart and barrels into me. He grapples me into a bear hug. "I'm so glad to see you."

I drop the fish so I can peel him off me. "Where are they?" I shake PJ by the shoulders.

"In the alley." His teeth rattle. His sunglasses slip to the end of his nose. "The dumpster."

Hopefully Finley still has his sunglasses on too. They'll protect him from Marilyn's tractor-beam eyes. I snag the fish off the ground in one hand and grab PJ's elbow in the other. I dash around the side of the building, tugging PJ along.

Clicks and whistles come out of the dumpster. A

rotten head of lettuce flies into the air and splats at my feet.

"Hold this." I thrust the packet of fish at PJ.

The clicking stops.

I take baby steps to the dumpster. PJ stays behind. I guess he's scared to look. I'm not feeling brave either, but I have to see. I have to know what that monster's done to my brother.

My hands press against cool metal. Streaks of rust are rough under my fingertips. I hold my breath and listen.

A low growl ricochets inside.

Stretching on my tiptoes isn't enough, the opening's too high. I can't see over the edge.

I wave PJ over. He can give me a boost. And his sunglasses. The last thing I want is to look into Marilyn's eyes without some protection.

He shuffles across the alley, making so much noise the whole world can hear him.

"You don't sneak around much do you?" No sense whispering now. She's gotta know we're here.

I show PJ how to lace his fingers together into a footstool. Like a wimp, he grumbles when I put my weight on him. I'm not even touching the bandages on his arm. I snatch his sunglasses, depositing them on my face, and then I rest my hand on his shoulder to steady myself. "OK. Hoist me up. Slowly."

When I peer over the edge of the dumpster, my breath catches.

STEP 13

Protect Mom

A LAMP STUCK ABOVE the "Employees Only" entrance, combined with the moon, casts enough light to see inside the dumpster. Although the sunglasses deepen the shadows and make everything look like a charcoal drawing.

There's Marilyn, scaly as ever, waist high in garbage with a mouth full of . . . brains.

Finley's submerged to his neck, his sunglasses perched on his hair, and that faraway look on his face same as when he was on PJ's diving board. His skull looks OK. So whose brains is she munching on? Unless she sucked his brains out his ear.

"You miserable monster. What have you done to him? I'll kill you. I will kill you!" Scrambling over the edge of the dumpster, I reach my hands out to grab Marilyn by the throat.

I miss and land splat on top of rotting vegetables. Like a stink bomb, the smell puffs around me, crawling up my nose. I sneeze. My eyes tear up. Now

Marilyn's blurrier through my smeared sunglasses.

She growls deep in her chest and spews saliva-drenched brains into my face and mouth.

"Ugh!" I spit and cough, forcing the brains back out. But I get their taste on my tongue and I scream, a girly scream that bounces off metal and escapes into the night sky.

"What's wrong?" Finley's voice cuts through the crazies strangling me from the inside out.

"Your brain. I just tasted your brain and it tastes like . . . cauliflower."

"That's 'cause it is cauliflower."

"Huh?" I grab his head and feel around the back and sides, careful not to squeeze too hard in case his empty skull collapses.

"Cut it out. I'm OK. Marilyn likes cauliflower. And broccoli, too." Finley's sunglasses have slipped back into place, and he sounds and acts like nothing strange is happening. He raises his hand from under the garbage and points. "Look."

Marilyn chomps on a bundle of celery still wrapped in plastic. She grins. Pieces stick to her pointy teeth.

WHACK. Squeal.

A door flung open. Rusty hinges.

"I thought I heard a kid scream," a woman says.

I know that voice.

Mom.

If she gets caught in Marilyn's hypno-stare, Marilyn's vegetarian moments are over for sure.

"Duck." I press down on Finley's head.

He must've recognized Mom's voice too. He doesn't argue and dives under a flattened box.

I roll a garbage bag stuffed full of who-knows-what on top of Marilyn.

She growls.

"Sh," I tell her as I hide under a busted crate. Fingers crossed PJ has enough sense to hide too.

Either Marilyn released a silent but deadly fart, or I'm inhaling a rancid salad. Doesn't really matter the source, the result is a lemon bar in my stomach threatening to crawl up my throat and join the party. I shift my face to the side, hoping for a clear space to breathe.

"Sounds like something's in the dumpster. I'll check it out." Footsteps clap the asphalt.

This is not good. Oh, Mom, turn around. Go back inside. Wood drags across blacktop, like she's moving something to stand on.

"What could've made that sound?" Her voice is

only a few feet above my head. She must be looking right at me. If she pokes around in the garbage . . .

I will myself still. Something slimy strokes my face. On Marilyn's side of me. I tighten my lips to keep from groaning.

Marilyn, don't take a bite out of me. Mom, go away. Finley, keep breathing, kiddo.

"Find anything, Molly?" a woman calls out.

"Must've been a cat. Bud needs to remember to keep this lid closed."

A clattering BANG rockets through my body. The boa constrictor of panic winds around my chest. Me and Finley are shut inside the dumpster. With Marilyn.

I can't hear footsteps. I can't tell if Mom is right outside or if she's gone back into the store. What I do hear is Marilyn next to my cheek.

"More food." Her wet breath spreads inside my ear.

"Agh!" I blast out of the garbage and hit the top of the dumpster with my fists.

A hand latches around my arm and starts tugging me down.

"Don't eat me." I flail in the dark, pounding on the lid. Something warm and sticky runs down the back of my neck. My own blood? I'm gonna die.

"She won't eat you," Finley says.

There's a steady pat-pat, pat-pat on the back of my shirt.

"Agh, she's touching me. Get her off. Get her off!"

"It's me. Finley."

Just when my racing heart steps on the breaks, the dumpster lid flies open. The moon bathes the garbage in gray light, and PJ pokes his head over the side. He must be standing on something, that or he slipped into two-inch heels.

"That lady went back inside. What's going on in here? Need help?" PJ extends his non-bandaged arm.

I grasp his wrist and forearm and use him like a climbing rope. "That wasn't a regular lady. That was my mom." I scramble out of the dumpster and knock PJ off a crate on my way down. "Come on. We gotta get Finley out of there." I reposition the crate, PJ gets back on, and I step up next to him.

"You've got something gross all over the back of you." He puts his hand where my hair meets my neck. When he pulls his fingers away, they're covered in oozy goo. He sniffs and then wipes the front of my shirt, leaving dark streaks. "Barbecue sauce."

"Thanks."

Finley stabs his hands up from the garbage, and me and PJ each grasp one of his arms. The crate wobbles, but I slam my foot down to keep it from pitching us off. Finley yanks, climbs, and heaves himself on top of the garbage heap. Using the box he was hiding underneath as a springboard, the momentum helps us pull him out.

Marilyn's still rummaging in the dumpster. And we can't leave her in there. Once she picks through it, she's gonna come looking for more. She'll figure out the food in the dumpster comes from the grocer's building next door. She'll go there next.

"She didn't eat you guys. That's great. Do you think her human-eating days are over?" PJ claps his hands, grinning.

"She didn't eat us because her mouth was already full. That's the trick. Keep those gnashing teeth busy and her mouth full. Go get the fish I brought."

While PJ retrieves the fish from the golf cart, I tell Finley my plan. "We'll use the fish to lure her out of the dumpster and away from the grocery store."

"Then what? When the sun comes up, won't she lose her legs? We gotta get her back to the pool before that happens." PJ hands me the fish packet.

"I got a better idea. We'll lead her to the ocean."

STEP 14

Lure the Mermaid

I UNWRAP THE BUNDLE and open one of the packets.

"Nice fish," Finley says. "Doesn't hardly smell like fish."

"I know, right?" That's 'cause it's fresh. It only stinks when it's gone bad."

PJ paces next to us, kicking up gravel.

I turn to yell at him to stop. That's when I notice he's wearing socks with his sandals. When we get out of this, I need to help this kid wise up. "I'll call her out."

"No. She doesn't like you." PJ grabs the fish and waves it over his head like he's flagging down an emergency vehicle.

"The feeling's mutual." Definitely. I will never like Marilyn. I can barely put up with PJ.

PJ ignores me and makes kissing sounds. "Come on out, Marilyn. More food. Come out, sweetie."

"That's disturbing." Finley shakes his head.

"I know, right?" I open another fish packet. "You

got your knife? We can cut a piece off and throw it in there. Give her a little taste." My Swiss Army knife's back at Zombie Cave. I should put a new one on Uncle George's list.

At least Finley's got his. He opens it and hands it to me. With some effort, I use the little knife to saw off hunks. "Here. Feed your pet."

PJ takes a piece and lobs it into the dumpster.

No response. All I hear are bugs humming around the alley light and a couple cars passing on the street.

"Give her another one."

PJ tosses in another piece while I cut more off.

This time the garbage rustles. A deep and guttural "More" escapes from the dumpster. The hairs on my arms spring to attention. I preferred when she didn't talk.

"Did you hear that? She likes it." PJ scoops up the rest of the fish pieces.

"Whoa. We need her to come out for them. Don't throw any more inside. Keep calling her out." She won't come for me. He's the one with the special bond. I just want to get her far away from this grocery store. Away from Mom.

"There's more food out here, Marilyn."

Now the dumpster sounds like a wolf pack is

scrounging inside.

"Marilyn?" PJ stands only a foot away from the dumpster.

Like a volcano erupting, garbage spews all over him, gook oozing from his hair like lava. I hope Mom doesn't come out to investigate the noise again.

Then Marilyn pops up like a jack-in-the-box, grabs PJ's shoulders, and yanks him into the dumpster with her. It happens so quick, I gotta rub my eyes.

"He's gone." Finley grabs my arm. His pulse beats through his palm. "She . . . took him." His grip starts to hurt. "She won't eat him, will she?"

"I–" I have to fight the urge to grab Finley and run home. Leave PJ to his pet. Let him figure it out. I didn't ask for this.

"Should we look inside?"

"Absolutely not." I'm not risking Finley. Or me. We're not going anywhere close to that dumpster now.

"It's all my fault. I fed his Sea-Monkeys the wrong food."

I imagine Finley's eyes are welling up underneath his sunglasses. I had no idea he was feeling so guilty. He's no guiltier than I am. I squeeze his hand, still gripping my arm. "It was an accident, for Pete's sake.

We didn't choose this."

But the little voice inside me says, *Yeah, but it is your choice if you run away and leave PJ behind. Could you live with that choice? Could Finley?*

Shoot! Me and PJ might not be best buds, but I sure don't want him devoured by a monster. He's not a bad kid. Snobby and selfish, yes. But not a total waste of space. "We gotta lead her to the ocean. Stick to the plan. You unwrap the fish, I'll cut."

While I saw and chop and rip the fish into pieces, I try not to listen for chow-time sounds from the dumpster, but I can't help it, my ears are tuned in. Luckily Marilyn's keeping quiet again. Maybe she's not going to eat PJ after all. Or maybe she swallowed him whole.

STEP 15

Race to the Sea

WE SET UP A TRAIL of fish parts from the dumpster to the alley entrance, and then I make Finley sit in the golf cart with the engine running.

"If anything happens to me, you leave as fast as you can."

"But, Mick—"

"Promise me."

"OK. I promise."

My days of tying him up to keep him out of trouble are over. I'm gonna have to trust him.

I hold the Swiss Army knife like a much larger, much better weapon. If Marilyn decides to snatch me too, she can count on a fight. I didn't survive Zombie Cave to get murdered by a mutant Sea-Monkey.

"This is it, you psychotic gorilla-woman. Come and get your fish."

Her webbed hands fling upward and grip the rim. Her claws scrape the metal, and all of a sudden,

I feel like a toddler in a diaper.

She pulls her head and shoulders up, and in one Ninja leap, she's crouched on the ground. A pink tongue slides across her pointy teeth. "More food."

Her eyes shimmer gray, not gold, thanks to PJ's sunglasses. She stands to her full height, as tall as Uncle George's six feet. Nanny Vargas's skirt cuts her bulging quads in half. Thick shins descend into huge feet. She's a scaly football player on steroids with six-pack abs and bursting biceps. PJ's sister's bikini top is stretched to the breaking point.

"Gosh, you are ugly." I back up. Sweat coats my skin like I just got out of the shower.

Marilyn bends and scrapes fish off the ground, cramming it into her mouth, slurping and chewing. Advancing.

The back of me hits—

Finley. "Get in," he says, tugging on my shirt.

I climb into the passenger seat.

Marilyn lunges at us, gargling a piece of fish. Her claws reach.

"Go. Go!"

Finley stomps on the gas pedal. The golf cart bucks, skids, and coughs. The gas gauge hovers above E. No time to stop at a gas station. We're too busy fleeing while I'm flinging fish into Marilyn's chest. Yes! She stops long enough for us to get some distance.

Then she's right behind us.

"She's fast." Fish slips through my fingers. Finally I grasp a glossy fish head and slap Marilyn in the face with it.

"There's cars at the stoplight. What do I do?"

"Sidewalk. Now. Turn right at the intersection. We'll go down Fogart Street."

The golf cart bumps over the curb and nearly tips, but I lean to the right. A kid inside a car gliding through the intersection slides his window down and points at us. The last thing we need is an audience. Hopefully his parents are normal and they won't believe him when he tells them what he saw.

Marilyn hurdles over the back of the golf cart into the seat behind me. "More food."

"Mick?"

"Keep driving. Make a left up ahead. Swing around the credit union." I grab fish pieces while I talk.

She gobbles them as fast as I throw them. We're going to run out. If only we could go faster. I know Finley's got the pedal to the floor. I should've bought more fish. I should've used the whole fifty dollars.

Back on the street, we pass the credit union and cruise down 5th. Most everyone must still be at the pavilion. Except Mr. Gee. His light's on in the Eclipse Comic Emporium, and I swear I see him look up from adjusting his front window display as we pass.

I can't worry about that now. I've got the last two pieces in my hands.

Marilyn eyeballs the raw fish like it's the last food on earth. It might as well be. And what do bloodthirsty mermaids do when the food's all gone? Eat the hand that feeds them.

The golf cart slows.

Sputters.

Stops.

The fuel gauge needle sits on E.

Marilyn growls.

We're in big trouble.

Marilyn snatches the last of the fish out of my hands and stuffs them into her mouth. Snarling, chewed bits and saliva spray from her lips.

I stare at my open palm. Air squeaks in my throat.

Spit drips down Marilyn's chin. "More."

"Heeee." In a world where a Sea-Monkey can turn into Marilyn, fish should magically appear when you need them most. But my palm remains empty.

"There's more in the ocean. Much more. That's where we're going. The ocean." Finley's tone is like he's talking to a two-year-old.

Marilyn cocks her head. So far, she's listening.

"You want to go see the ocean, don't you? And see all the fish? Lots more food." Finley gets out of the golf cart. Slowly.

I get out too. *Steady, remember to breathe.*

From either side, me and Finley meet by the headlights. Marilyn crouches in the back of the golf cart, staring at us.

Five more blocks and we'll hit parking lot. A block later, it's wide-open sand. We can do it. We can do it. We both got our gym shoes on and enough adrenaline to climb Mt. Everest.

"Run!" I yell.

We spin. We sprint.

And before you can say, "What were you thinking, you numbskull?" Marilyn's flung me over her shoulder. Hot breath coats the back of my legs.

Finley lands with a "Humph" on her other shoulder, and the two of us drape over her back like two sides of a cape, butts saluting the moon.

I know I should say rumpuses instead of butts.

Consider this a verbal emergency.

"Where are you taking us?" All I can see is pavement. And Marilyn's scaly back. Hair everywhere. The stringy hair growing out of her head whips my face and gets in my mouth. "Pth-tooey."

"Maybe she's taking us to the beach."

"How?" I spit hair. "Does she know the way?"

"It's like the grocery store. I pictured how to get there in my head, and she went."

I have mixed up feelings about Marilyn reading minds. It's good 'cause when I was planning on running, I pretty much mapped out the way to the beach. It's bad 'cause Marilyn would know all the times I planned to get rid of her. That would explain why she doesn't like me.

"Clear your mind of everything except the fish in the ocean. Maybe it'll motivate her not to drown and eat us when we get there."

Wherever we're going, we're going fast. Imagine a sprinter on triple-fast play. Her feet hardly touch the ground. Me and Finley hardly bounce. She is, however, leaving a trail of slime, just like PJ said. Snail slime.

And Finley is right too. Once Marilyn stops, we're at the beach. She flings us into the sand like bundles of beach gear. The moon cuts a runway strip to the ocean and out to the horizon. My sunglasses make everything black and gray, but I'm sure the light is silver. I don't dare peek. Now that I'm near the water, it would be too easy for her to hypno-drown me.

"Keep your sunglasses on, Finley."

"It's awfully dark."

"You'll get used to it. Stay put. We'll see what she does."

Marilyn walks over the tidal zone like she's walking down the aisle at her wedding. From behind, in the dark, she looks almost normal. As normal as any six-foot, lady body builder in teeny-tiny clothes.

She stops and looks to her right. She's staring at something. Must be a rock or hill of sand left from someone digging.

Until it stands and brushes itself off. "Hey there. Don't see many folks this part of the beach at night. Is the concert over?" The figure trounces through the sand right up to Marilyn with his hand extended. "Name's Karl Wheetly. And you are?"

Let Them Go

"KARL! NO. STAY AWAY from her." I leapfrog over the sand until I catch my balance, then I run full speed, Finley at my heels.

"Mick? That you?"

But like a nightmare where you run down a hallway that keeps stretching and you keep getting nowhere, I can't get to Karl in time.

Marilyn's got him by the shoulders. She spins him so he looks at her. His whole body relaxes, and he falls into her arms like she's his girlfriend.

"Is she gonna kiss him?"

"No way." I keep running. A kiss would be gross enough. That's no kiss.

Her mouth opens so big you can fit a basketball inside. Her jaw has dislocated or something. The skin below her cheeks stretches. She's gonna eat him.

I stop in my tracks. Finley slams into me, almost knocking us both down.

Marilyn does the most creepy, amazing thing I've ever seen in my whole entire life. A huge, slimy bubble slips out of her mouth and wraps around Karl's head. Marilyn's body expands and contracts like she's breathing hard, pumping air. The bubble gets bigger and bigger, encasing the entire top half of Karl.

Finley pulls his glasses down onto the tip of his nose.

"Don't. It's not safe." I try to push them back up.

Finley bats my hand away. "You gotta see this." He pulls my glasses down.

In the moonlight the bubble is shades of silver instead of mottled gray. It spins and trembles as it grows, like a giant soap bubble, the silhouette of Karl Wheetly trapped inside.

"Can you smell it?" I choke back a cough.

"Uh-huh." Finley's mouth is hanging open, eyes huge in his head, same as when he first saw PJ's rec room.

Smells like rotting garbage, fish, SPAM, and whatever else wound up in Marilyn's stomach today.

"Look, she's done." Finley points.

Marilyn's jaw is back in place. She steps away from her creation: a man-sized bubble with a man inside.

"You think he's OK in there?" Finley slides his glasses back up.

I push mine up too. "Yeah, I do." The big question is, why'd she put him in a bubble? Could be she's like a spider wrapping him up for later.

"Maybe PJ's in a bubble too."

It's easy for me to put two and two together when Finley makes so much sense. "And Nanny Vargas and Pool Guy."

"And Gene," we say together.

They could be all alive and inside bubbles! Me and Finley grab arms and jump in a circle like little kids. Maybe she didn't eat them. Maybe she didn't drown them. Maybe . . . Marilyn screeches, sending me and Finley to our knees, hands over our ears. She towers over us, grabs us each by the shirt collar, yanks us to our feet. "More food."

Something I didn't count on: teaching Marilyn how to fish.

Without releasing our shirts, she drags us to the lapping shoreline. Without nets I can't catch any fish for her. Digging up bean clams and mole crabs is an option, but if I know Marilyn, they'll only disappoint her. I'll end up in a bubble of my own. She could swallow me in her expando-gullet out of spite.

"You gotta catch your food yourself now." Finley pat-pats her arm. "You can live in the ocean now, eat as much as you want, but you gotta catch it yourself."

Marilyn clicks and squeaks. Then she strokes Finley's hand still resting on her arm. "Come with."

"Oh no. Not going to happen."

She whacks me across the chest, and I land with my back in the wet sand three feet away from her.

I struggle to stand. "You can't have him." I lower my head and barrel at her full force.

She whacks me again.

"Stop it!" Finley hollers. "You can't beat up everybody to get your own way."

I stay on the ground this time, taking in the fact that my little brother just scolded me. Me. Feels worse than getting pummeled by a mermaid with legs.

Marilyn clicks and whistles.

"You have to make new friends, Marilyn. I bet you'll like dolphins." He slips his hand around her webby talons. "Come on. I'll take you partway, but then I gotta go home."

"Home."

"That's right. This is your home now." He leads her into the water.

I clench the sand. I want to grab Finley out of the ocean so bad. He can't swim. She'll pull him under. Take him with her. "Finley, please."

"I'm OK. I got this." He wades out, the sea calm with the smallest of breakers, Marilyn holding his hand.

He's waist-deep when Marilyn grasps him in a hug. My throat squeezes and I can't scream. Can't get air.

She lets him go. Cocks her head and listens.

I listen too.

There's clicking and squeaking coming from the ocean, and it's not Marilyn. Just past the crest of the surf where the water is black glass, I see the head and shoulders of a person treading water.

Marilyn clicks, squeals, whistles.

The figure repeats the same sounds.

My throat clears and I think I say, "Wow." I stand and take off the sunglasses to get a better view.

Whoever's swimming out there glides into the moonlight, skin pale and shimmering, hair like liquid silver, and I realize who I'm looking at. Mr. Wheetly's mermaid.

Marilyn drops Finley's left hand, squeals once, and plunges headfirst into the water. Finley stands frozen, his sunglasses in his right hand. She must've put him in a trance.

I rush out to him, splashing like a dufus.

When I reach him, he's grinning. "She's got a friend. How cool is that?"

Out in the ocean, Marilyn and the mermaid greet each other with whistles and squeaks. They dive below the surface together and disappear.

"She didn't look back." Finley sounds sad.

I'm not particularly happy myself. I mean, I'm glad Marilyn's gone, but I always thought Finley looked up to me. After what he said about my hurting people to get what I want, maybe I was wrong. "I'm sorry."

"Yeah. She has a new friend. One her own size. She won't have to make bubbles anymore. I knew she'd be OK."

"I'm not sorry about Marilyn. About us." I want to squeeze his shoulder. I don't. I need to say it so I know for sure he understands. The words are hard. "I'm sorry I made you doubt me."

He hugs me. "I'm not mad at you. You're the best brother ever."

I hug him back and swing him around. We walk out of the water. The inside of our shoes squish with each step. "You don't need so much protecting anymore, do you?"

"Nope."

"Is it OK if I still keep an eye on you? Mom'll want me to."

"S'OK." He stops for a minute to kick a piece of driftwood from our path. "You know, if you keep your fists in your pockets, you can't punch anyone."

"That's a good idea. I'll try that next time. You know what else is a good idea?"

"What?"

"Getting Karl Wheetly out of that bubble."

Pop A Bubble

THE BUBBLE ENDS UP being more like a thick shell of see-through peanut brittle. I stab at it with Finley's Swiss Army knife. And stab. And stab. Until I got a hole. Me and Finley break pieces off. Sometimes the little blade helps. Sometimes we use only our hands. Takes a while. Finally the hole's big enough for us to crawl inside one at a time. We stoop next to Karl, who stands in the middle where the bubble curves upward.

He's covered in sticky goo like he rolled around in a bed of boogers.

I poke him. "Karl? You OK?"

He just stands there in a trance, eyes glazed like a dead fish. His chest moves and wheezy breaths pipe through his nose.

From inside the bubble, the sound of the ocean is muffled. The goop coating this side of the bubble oozes and swirls. The air is moist like Marilyn's hot breath. Feels creepy.

"Let's get outta here."

Me and Finley push and pull Karl out of the hole we made. He follows blindly. Crackling and popping chase us, and when I turn to look at the bubble, it crumples inward. All that's left is a pile of gooey shards for the tide to carry away.

Karl sits in the sand, facing the sea.

"When's he gonna snap out of it?" Finley asks.

"No clue."

There's a kid's bucket and shovel nearby. I take the bucket to the ocean's edge, fill 'er up, and run back, water sloshing against the sides. "Sorry, Karl, but you need to wake up." I toss the seawater into his face.

"What the—" He scrubs his eyes with his fists. "Mick?" He coughs. "Why am I wet? What's this gunk all over me?"

I'm too shocked to respond. When I threw the water at Karl Wheely, it splashed over and around him and onto Marilyn's bubble rubble. Once the bubble was broken into pieces, well, the water made the pieces melt. Now all that's left is a puddle of shiny goop on the sand.

"You tripped and fell, Mr. Wheely. Knocked yourself out," Finley takes over for me. "Mick poured water on you to wake you up."

"Whoa." Karl tries to push himself off the ground.

Me and Finley each grab on and help.

He wavers a bit and rubs his temple. "Must've hit my head. Got a bit of a headache."

"Where's your truck? We can help you get to it." I hope he drove. We sure can't bring him home in the dead golf cart.

He stands straighter, color seeping back into his cheeks. "It's just over that berm. Not even sure why I came out here tonight. Last thing I remember, I was driving home from Mac's Tavern. I only drank coffee with Sam Reed, I swear."

We start walking. Karl's strides get more confident as we go. Eventually Finley and me have to jog to stay even with him.

"What're you two doing out at the beach so late? Not that I'm complaining. Glad you were here." He swipes his hand down his arm and flicks the slime off his fingers. "Did I fall into a pile of fish guts, or what? Stuff stinks to high heaven."

"We were going to catch the last of the concert." I sure can't tell him we were releasing a mutant Sea-Monkey into the wild.

"The golf cart ran out of gas," Finley adds.

"So we walked to the beach instead. Thought maybe we'd find somebody night fishing." From here I can see Mr. Wheetly's truck a few steps away. The paint brightens under the full moon, making it look show-room new.

"I've got a gas can. Least I can do is get your cart going again." The walk in the salty air seems to have livened him back to normal. He's perky again. "I know. No rides with strangers." He pulls the red can from the back of his truck. The gas sloshes. "How far to your cart? I'll carry the gas."

I remember Marilyn carrying us for blocks. The golf cart is far. A couple miles at least.

"You're not a stranger, Mr. Wheetly. You pulled us out of the ocean this summer. You took us to shore in your boat, remember?" Finley grins. "That already counts as a ride."

"Of course I remember. But this is your big brother here. Let's defer to him. What do you say, Mick? Want a ride?"

"You bet I do."

Make Amends

PJ SETTLES INTO THE LEATHER upholstery across from me. "I miss her."

Gene's reflected eyebrow rises in the rearview mirror. He looks like he wants to say something, but he shakes his head instead.

I say it for him. "She didn't stick you inside a slime-filled bubble and store you at the bottom of the swimming pool."

"She liked kids." He blinks fast to keep the tears inside his eyes.

Hopefully they stay there. PJ's blubber-fests over Marilyn are crazy uncomfortable. When Finley told him Marilyn swam off with her new mermaid friend, he sobbed like he'd been deserted. I guess he sorta was.

"I wish I could've said goodbye. I wish you didn't leave me in the dumpster."

"I told you. We had to lead her away from you. We thought she would try to eat you. We thought she might've already eaten you. Don't forget, she chased me and Finley all the way through town. We did come back for you."

"Yeah. You did."

"Look, it's over. Nanny doesn't remember anything. Nick the Pool Guy doesn't remember anything."

"Heat exhaustion," Gene pipes up. "That week it did hit 102 degrees Fahrenheit." The stoplight turns green, and he eases through the intersection.

"They think they passed out from the heat," I confirm.

"Nanny's still embarrassed we all saw her wearing just a slip." PJ's face isn't all blotchy, and he stopped tearing up. He's finally coming around.

"We were just trying to cool her off," I say. "She never needs to know her skirt swam out to sea. The only people who know what really happened are the three of us and Finley."

"And I'm not saying bubkes." Gene steers the car onto Benton Street.

"No one's gonna track her down. She's hanging with her mer-friends. It's all good."

PJ sighs. "I know."

"Plus you're not grounded anymore for staining the pool. If you ask me," I give his shoulder a little punch, "I think black grout looks cool."

Gene slides the sedan up to the curb in front of Eclipse Comic Emporium. "We're here, boys."

"Come on. This will cheer you up." As soon as I open the door, heat fights against the air conditioning and wins.

PJ follows me out, sweat popping on his forehead. "Thanks for driving, Gene," he calls out before shutting the door behind him.

"Listen to you. Mr. Nice Guy now."

PJ shrugs. "What if none of them like me?"

"They'll like you. Trust me." The bells above the door jingle while I hold it open for PJ.

"Hey, kids. They're in the storage room." Mr. Gee gestures toward a beaded curtain. "Gotta take care of these customers, so you'll have to introduce yourselves." He directs his attention back to the couple at the cash register.

Pink and purple beads rattle as PJ and me pass through the doorway. Selena Kitty rubs her side against my ankle and then winds around PJ's feet.

"That's a good sign." Selena Kitty's tail curls when PJ scratches the sweet spot between her shoulders. "You're good with cats."

PJ smiles.

Selena Kitty gives him a long chin rub and then darts under a table covered with a thick blanket. High-pitched mews pierce the cloth.

I lift the corner of the blanket, and six kittens tumble from underneath the table. PJ sits and kittens crawl on his lap, climb his shirt, tug at his laces.

"Oh man. How am I gonna decide? I want them all. Which one do you like?"

I pick up the shaggy gray one. "This one's kinda cute. Looks like a ball of dryer lint with a pink nose."

"I like that one too. How 'bout this one?" He holds a squirmy tabby. "Or this one with the green eyes. What one do you think Finley would like?"

"All of them," I decide. In fact, if Finley were here, he'd probably convince me to sneak one into our apartment. Good thing he's at the YMCA today. Uncle George splurged on a family membership, and Finley's learning to swim at last. In a pool with life-guards.

A black kitten with a white muzzle and four white paws scales PJ's back. She sits atop his shoulder and purrs like a motorized scooter.

"I think this one's picked you."

PJ snorts when the kitten pokes her paw into his ear.

"Mr. Gee said they're all girl cats, so you have to pick a girl's name."

One word starts to form on PJ's lips. An M word. Before he can say it, I cut him off. "No. Absolutely. Not. Marilyn."

PJ laughs. "I was gonna name her Mittens, you dork."

And I laugh too.

Mick, Finley, and PJ's List of Materials
ALSO KNOWN AS WHAT WE LEARNED TO HAVE WITH US NEXT TIME

1. Clearly labeled Sea-Monkey food, duh!
2. Sunglasses, for deflecting hypno-rays.
3. A harpoon and a net. (OK, PJ, OK, never mind about that.)
4. More than one Swiss Army knife, for cutting through mermaid bubbles.
5. Towels, for wiping mermaid goo.
6. A continuous supply of canned meat, especially SPAM—a mermaid favorite.
7. Fresh fish. Lots of fresh fish.
8. Rotten vegetables. Who knew, right?
9. A golf cart.
10. Fencing uniforms, to protect skin from claws.
11. A book about mermaid lore, for reference. Finley's idea, a good one, right?
12. A large "No Adults Allowed" sign. Really, it's for their own good.
13. An alternative pet. Something sweet, warm, and fuzzy. For attachment purposes.

Come Visit Us at
www.SlugPieStories.com

Help vote for the next Slug Pie Story
Send in your fan art
Share zombie killing tips and tricks
Print Mick's favorite family recipes
Learn more about your favorite Slug Pie Story
characters
And more . . .

While Mick's story is fresh in your mind, would you leave us a review in your favorite review spot?

Goodreads: www.goodreads.com
Amazon: www.amazon.com
Barnes & Noble: www.BN.com
Books A Million: www.booksamillion.com

ACKNOWLEDGEMENTS

This book could not have been created without help and inspiration from the following:

The Blaski Family and The Hockhalter Family for their emotional and financial support.

The extraordinary Jennifer Kay and Alice Fleury for their critiquing, and writerly love.

The Asner Family, The Morris Family, The Beasley Family, Sharon Cooper, and The Munson Family for their readerly love.

Michael Carr for first believing.

Rachel Defries, Corinne Dyuvis, and Katie Carson for holding hands online during the rollercoaster ride.

Amy Maddox for editing and proofreading with scalpel precision and tender care.

Kat Powell for her exceptional talent, unending patience, and kick-rumpus illustrations.

Nick, Clarissa, and Irina for never-ending curiosity and enthusiasm.

For the writers, too numerous to mention them all, who put themselves out there every day, teaching and inspiring the rest of us.

To the readers. You are the reason.

CPSIA information can be obtained
at www.ICGtesting.com
Printed in the USA
LVHW010421291018
595166LV00006B/151/P

9 780990 380139